CHEERLEADERS

#42

FIGHTING BACK

CAROL ELLIS

D1002744

SCHOLASTIC INC.
New York Toronto London Auckland Sydney

Scholastic Books are available at special discounts for quantity purchases for use as premiums, promotional items, retail sales through specialty market outlets, etc. For details contact: Special Sales Manager, Scholastic Inc., 730 Broadway, New York, NY 10003.

ISBN 0-590-41628-6

12 11 10 9 8 7 6 5 4 3 2 1   8 9/8 0 1 2 3/9

Printed in the U.S.A.   01

First Scholastic printing, June 1988

FIGHTING BACK

CHEERLEADERS

Trying Out	Rivals
Getting Even	Proving It
Rumors	Going Strong
Feuding	Stealing Secrets
All the Way	Taking Over
Splitting	Spring Fever
Flirting	Scheming
Forgetting	Falling in Love
Playing Games	Saying Yes
Betrayed	Showing Off
Cheating	Together Again
Staying Together	Saying No
Hurting	Coming Back
Living It Up	Moving Up
Waiting	Changing Loves
In Love	Acting Up
Taking Risks	Talking Back
Looking Good	All or Nothing
Making It	Getting Serious
Starting Over	Having It All
Pulling Together	Fighting Back

CHAPTER

"The Wolves got a basket
  And it looked so fine!
  We think they ought to do it
  One more time!"

The six members of Tarenton High School's
varsity cheerleading squad, their red-and-white
uniforms a flash of color in the center of the gym
floor, raised their voices and urged the fans to
shout along. The fans didn't need to be asked
twice; their roaring, stamping, and clapping
shook the bleachers and filled the gym with
sound.

"The Wolves have the ball
  And they're starting to shine!
  We think they ought to sink it
  One more time!"

1

In the middle of all the shouting, the sound of the game itself was completely lost. The basketball might as well have been made of cotton for all the noise it made as it was bounced along the floor and slammed against the backboards. Noiseless as it was, though, no one lost sight of it, especially the Tarenton Wolves. As the clock wound down to the final seconds of the game, Tarenton's center captured the ball, dribbled it briskly down the court, and dunked it into the basket one more time. The Wolves had beaten the Deep River Killers, 44 to 30. A few more wins like this one and they might have a shot at the state championship.

Up in the stands, Mary Ellen Tilford hugged her husband, Pres, and then clapped loudly as the team and the cheerleading squad streamed happily toward the locker rooms. "The squad looked great!" she shouted over the cheers and whistles of the fans. "And that new cheer is fantastic. Every time we come to a game, I get this incredible urge to go out there and do cartwheels with them."

Pres smiled and took her hand as they made their way down to the gym floor. "Why don't you try it sometime?" he asked, his brown eyes teasing. "I'd love to see the look on Coach Engborg's face."

Mary Ellen tossed her blonde hair back and shook her head. "I said it was an urge," she laughed. "I didn't say I couldn't control it. Anyway, Coach Engborg wouldn't just look at me, she'd tie me up and throw me out of town."

Both former Tarenton High cheerleaders, Pres

and Mary Ellen had first-hand experience with Ardith Engborg's intense commitment to the precision of her varsity squad. Nothing short of a major catastrophe was allowed to interfere with it, and the Tilfords knew that an "urge" to do cartwheels and stag leaps again wouldn't meet the coach's standards. And, actually, neither one of them wanted to turn back the clock. Since graduating from high school and getting married, they were leading very fulfilling lives: Pres, working for his wealthy father's manufacturing company; Mary Ellen, studying at the local college and modeling part-time at a fashionable boutique. Working, studying, and building a marriage filled their days.

Still, they hadn't lost touch with the squad, and they didn't want to. As often as they could, they went to the games and watched the cheerleaders go through their routines, some of which Mary Ellen and Pres had done themselves. And it was always exciting to see a new routine, like tonight's "One More Time." The squad was as good as it had ever been, and Pres and Mary Ellen felt proud of having been part of it.

Tonight, though, Pres was tired and couldn't work up as much enthusiasm as Mary Ellen. His job at his father's company required long, demanding hours, and today had been one of the longest and most demanding. What he really wanted to do was go home, but Mary Ellen was full of energy and wanted to see the squad, so he followed her out of the gym and down the hall, hoping she wouldn't stay talking too long.

"Congratulations!" Mary Ellen called out

3

when she saw the cheerleaders in the milling crowd outside the locker room doors. "You guys looked spectacular."

Olivia Evans, the squad's small, dynamic captain, laughed and gave Mary Ellen a hug. "I thought I saw you two up there," she said. "And thanks for the compliment. Isn't the new cheer great? Melissa choreographed it," she added, nodding toward the slender, brown-haired girl who was listening intently to something Coach Engborg was saying to her. The team's alternate cheerleader, Melissa Brezneski rarely got to perform, but she'd already put her mark on the squad by choreographing new cheers that combined the vigor of gymnastics with the grace of ballet. This came naturally to Melissa, who had studied ballet since she was a little girl.

"Too bad she didn't get the chance to do her own cheer," Pres said.

"Don't worry, she'll get a chance." Tara Armstrong, her long red hair damp with perspiration, joined them. "One of these days, one of us will come down with the flu and Melissa will step in."

"Coach Engborg lets you off for the flu now?" Mary Ellen pretended to look shocked. "In our day, it had to be the plague, at least." She laughed and shook her head. "She must be getting soft."

"Soft?" Sean Dubrow, one of the two boys on the squad, raised his eyebrows. "We were still working on that cheer five minutes before game time." Glancing over at the coach and Melissa, he shook his head. "Looks like Coach Engborg is making a few suggestions. She probably thinks

4

we could work in some more handsprings and herky jumps if we just try a little harder." He grinned, his dark eyes twinkling. "I say we get out of here before she makes us go through it 'one more time.' "

Everyone laughed. They'd all been exaggerating, of course, about how tough Ardith Engborg was. She *was* tough, but she was also fair. She'd never call a practice after a game. Of course, she'd definitely call one before a game, if she thought they needed it. So even though it was Friday night, and they were all eager to shower, change, and leave the school, they waited to hear what the coach had to say.

After a couple of minutes, Coach Engborg finished talking to Melissa and glanced up, a smile tugging at the corners of her mouth as she saw the cheerleaders trying not to look impatient. "Melissa and I spotted one or two places in the new routine that we'd like to change," she said. "Since it's not anything that can be done overnight, Melissa's going to spend the next few days on it. You did good work," she went on, her smile getting bigger. "See you at the game tomorrow night."

"No practice tomorrow?" Sean sounded as if he couldn't quite believe it.

"Not unless you want to call one," the coach said dryly, heading for the door.

"Go ahead, Sean," Peter Rayman, the other boy on the squad, teased. "Call a practice and see what it's like to have five friends suddenly become your enemies."

"Olivia's the captain," Hope Chang pointed out quickly. "She's the one to call a Saturday practice."

"Right," Jessica Bennett agreed, smiling hopefully at Olivia. "And you wouldn't do that, would you?"

"Well . . ." Olivia sighed and pretended to think it over seriously. Then she grinned. "I guess as long as we warm up half an hour before game time, we can skip it, just this once."

Sean threw his arms into the air. "A free Saturday!" he shouted. "I say if the Wolves win the game tomorrow, we celebrate. How about a party? In fact, how about a party even if they don't win?"

It had been a while since the last squad party, and the others agreed enthusiastically. Unfortunately, a quick discussion revealed that no one's house was free, not even Sean's, whose widowed father was usually out on a date on Saturday nights. "I guess I spoke too soon," Sean said. "Dad's got a business trip coming up, and his plane leaves at 5:30 Sunday morning. He said he's going to bed with the chickens, so I don't think he'd be too understanding if we blasted him awake with rock music."

"Well, why don't we just go get a pizza together?" Hope suggested.

"We do that all the time," Jessica said. "Maybe we should just put the party off. I might be able to get permission to use my house next weekend."

"Don't put it off," Mary Ellen said quickly. "How about our place? Pres and I have plenty of room and we're ready for a party, right, Pres?"

"Sure . . . right." Pres smiled. Inside, though, he was slightly annoyed. Throwing their house open for a party was something he and Mary Ellen should discuss, he thought. *Beforehand.* "Well, I guess we'll see everybody tomorrow night, then," he said, trying to sound welcoming. "Win or lose."

Thanking the Tilfords, the cheerleaders broke apart and went off to shower and change, while Pres and Mary Ellen headed outside for their car. With one look at Pres's face, Mary Ellen could tell that something was bothering him. "What's wrong?" she asked as they pulled out of the parking lot. "Are you mad or something?"

"I'm not mad," Pres said. "I just wish we could have talked about this party before you decided to give it. The house is a mess, you know."

Mary Ellen laughed. "So? No one's going to be checking for dust. We'll shove things in closets and under the bed and do one of our super-quick cleanups."

"You mean *I'll* do one of our super-quick cleanups," Pres said. "You're working at Marnie's tomorrow, remember?"

"Oh, is that the problem?" Mary Ellen sat up a little straighter. "That you have to clean up on your own?"

"No, it's not," Pres said, wishing he'd never mentioned housecleaning. "I just think having a party is something we should decide together. I mean, what if I wasn't in the mood for one? Or what if I wanted to do something else?"

"Well, do you?"

"That's not the point." Pres turned the Porsche

off the main street and onto the winding road that led to their house. "The point is," he went on, "that you have a habit of planning things without letting me in on them first."

Until then, Mary Ellen had been ready to laugh. It seemed like a dumb argument to be having, and she knew she could joke him out of it. But once he said, "you have a habit," she wasn't so amused anymore. Pres was exaggerating; she'd only planned one or two things without telling him first. And anyway, he had his habits, too, like making a big deal out of nothing, which is exactly what this was.

As he pulled into the drive of their carriage house, Pres glanced sideways at Mary Ellen and saw that her mouth was pulled down in a frown. When was he ever going to learn to pick the right time for a discussion like this? He'd made her angry and if he tried to apologize now, she'd only get angrier. With a sigh, he decided to drop the whole thing until tomorrow.

On her side of the car, Mary Ellen was fighting the urge to say something sarcastic. It was tempting, but she knew it wouldn't do any good. It would just turn a small disagreement into a big fight. Better let it ride until tomorrow, she told herself. By tomorrow, everything will be all right.

"Tomorrow night," said Tara Armstrong. At home in her bedroom, Tara shifted the phone to her other hand and pulled another pillow under her head. It was late and she'd been in bed for an hour already, willing herself to stay awake in case Patrick Henley, her fiance, found a minute to

8

call her. Just as she was about to give up and turn out the bedside lamp, he'd finally called. But she could tell he was busy and distracted, and she knew they wouldn't be able to talk long. "A party at Pres and Mary Ellen's after the game," she went on, wanting to tell him about it in case she didn't see him tomorrow. "Do you think you'll be able to make it?" She waited. "Patrick?"

On the other end of the line, Patrick cleared his throat. "Sorry," he said. "I had to sign a delivery sheet. What's this about a party?"

Tara smiled and shook her head. Patrick's business — the Henley TLC Moving Company — was booming, and that was great. But sometimes she wished it wouldn't boom on Friday and Saturday nights. "It's at Pres and Mary Ellen's after the game tomorrow," she said again. "And I'm inviting you, of course. Can you come?"

"Wait a second," Patrick said. Again, there was a pause. Tara could hear a whispered conversation and the rattle of papers. Yawning, she stretched out her hand and stroked the soft tiger-striped fur of Tabitha, the kitten Patrick had given her. Tabby purred like an engine but didn't open her eyes, and Tara yawned again, letting her own eyes close. It was late, she was sleepy, and Patrick was obviously busy. She smiled drowsily, thinking of how handsome his face was when he was concentrating on something.

"Sorry again," Patrick's voice said, after about five minutes. "We're just about finished here, and I think — I'm not sure — but I think I can make the party."

There was no answer.

9

"Tara?" Patrick waited, listening closely, and then he smiled into the phone as he heard the unmistakable sound of quiet, steady breathing. Tara was fast asleep.

"I couldn't believe it!" Tara said the next day. "I actually fell asleep on him in the middle of a telephone conversation. And when I tried to call him this morning to apologize, he was already out on a job."

Mary Ellen laughed. "Don't worry about it," she advised. "I fell asleep while Pres was talking to me once. And we were in the same room. Now *that* was embarrassing!"

It was Saturday, and the two girls were at the Pinelands Mall. Having studied until one that afternoon, finally finishing a paper for social studies, Tara had decided to reward herself by buying a new outfit. Getting new clothes was something she used to do almost as regularly as brushing her teeth, but lately she'd been spending a lot less time adding to her already vast wardrobe. The contents of her closet just didn't seem as important as they once had, and she knew it was mostly because of Patrick. Not that he didn't care what she looked like, he just cared more about who she was.

But that didn't mean Tara had lost interest in clothes — a phenomenon she knew would never occur. Now that she had a free Saturday afternoon, she would make the most of it. By three-thirty, she'd found a pair of soft, rust-colored velveteen pants, a creamy silk blouse, and open-toed, sling-back shoes that matched the pants.

She was going to look terrific at the party, whether Patrick could come or not, but just in case he did come, she decided to get something extra-special. The best place to do that was at Marnie's Boutique, and that's where she'd run into Mary Ellen, who was just changing back into her street clothes after modeling the latest fashions most of the day.

Mary Ellen knew how to dress as well as anyone, and she showed Tara a pair of delicate hairclips that were shaped like butterflies and sparkled with tiny rhinestones and colored beads. Tara bought them, put them in her hair immediately, and then joined Mary Ellen for some more shopping.

The two of them had had a great time trying on clothes, browsing through the bookstore, and buying bright yellow paper plates and cups for the party. Now they were sitting in a sandwich shop, having a Coke before heading home.

"I guess falling asleep wasn't such a terrible thing to do," Tara agreed, "but I bet I get teased about it for at least a week."

"Make it a month," Mary Ellen joked. "That's how long it was before Pres let me forget about it. He still mentions it once in a while." Then she sighed, thinking of Pres and last night's argument. They hadn't talked about it this morning, mainly because they hadn't had time to talk at all. Before going to Marnie's she had to get to the library, so while Pres was still in the shower, she'd gulped some coffee and rushed out.

Mary Ellen still thought Pres was wrong about her "habit" of planning things without consulting him, and she was going to tell him so as soon as she got home. Okay, maybe she shouldn't have invited everybody over to their house like that, but if he'd wanted to do something else, all he had to do was say so. The kids on the squad wouldn't have been insulted. After all, they weren't business acquaintances, they were friends. The fact that he didn't have anything else he wanted to do proved that he'd picked an argument just to make a point.

"Uh-oh," Tara said, breaking into Mary Ellen's thoughts, "I'd better get going. My bus comes in five minutes."

"Why are you taking the bus?"

"My car's in for a tune-up," Tara explained. "Dad dropped me off here on his way to the health club, but he said he wouldn't be able to come and get me. And Mother's at the hairdresser's. They're going to a big dinner party tonight."

"I can give you a lift home," Mary Ellen said, pushing back her chair. "Come on. All I have to do is get some coffee beans at the Gourmet Shop and we're on our way."

It seemed like half the population of Tarenton had decided to buy something at the Gourmet Shop, and by the time Mary Ellen and Tara got out, it was 5:30. Instead of going home and then having to call somebody else for a ride to the game, Tara decided to have Mary Ellen drop her off at the high school.

While Tara called Marie, the Armstrongs' live-in housekeeper, to tell her she wouldn't be home until after the game and party, Mary Ellen wandered by a group of booths set up in the main entrance of the mall. As her eyes roved over the displays of handmade jewelry and dried flower arrangements, she suddenly spotted something that made her laugh. One of the vendors was selling a collection of buttons with sayings printed on them, and one of the buttons — a bright orange one — said "Love Beats All." Mary Ellen smiled to herself as she bought it and pinned it on the front of her jacket. There's more than one way to prove a point, she thought.

Then Tara joined her, the butterfly clips glinting in her coppery red hair. "What's that supposed to mean?" she asked, pointing to the button.

"It's a private joke," Mary Ellen laughed. "I hope."

Arms full of shopping bags, the two girls made their way down to the mall's cavernous underground parking garage. Mary Ellen's car was by itself in a dark, distant corner of the lowest level.

"Sorry it's so far away," she said. "When I got here, the garage was packed. I was lucky to find this spot. Now look — the place is practically empty."

With footsteps echoing off the cement floor, they reached the car, dumped their packages into the trunk, and slid into the front seat.

"Are you coming to the game?" Tara asked, reaching for her seatbelt.

"I'm not sure," Mary Ellen put the key in the ignition and turned it. "I guess it depends on how — "

"On what?" Tara asked.

Mary Ellen didn't answer.

Tara stopped fumbling with the seatbelt and looked across to the driver's side. One hand on the wheel, one on the gear shift, Mary Ellen's eyes were locked on the rearview mirror. It was dim and shadowy in this corner of the garage, but even in the semidarkness, Tara could read the expression on her friend's face. Mary Ellen was terrified.

"What is it?" Tara asked. "What's wrong?"

Mary Ellen's eyes never left the mirror.

Quickly, Tara turned and looked behind her. And then she understood. Someone was with them in the car. Someone with a face made hideous and distorted by a nylon stocking. Someone with a gun in his hand, pointed straight at Mary Ellen's head.

CHAPTER

Alone in the Tarenton High gym, Melissa Brezneski punched a button on her portable recorder and waited for the tape to rewind. For two hours, she'd been going over and over a single movement in the new cheer, trying to make it fit, and she thought she might finally have it right.

Listening to the hissing tape, she smiled at what her mother had said about her coming over here on a Saturday afternoon. "The gym?" Mrs. Brezneski had looked baffled. "But honey, you won't even get a chance to perform that cheer. I thought you'd be using the time to practice your ballet."

Not too long ago, when Melissa used to eat, sleep, and breathe ballet, that would have been true. She would have been at the rehearsal room downtown, working at the barre and dreaming of the day when she'd be a professional ballerina. That dream hadn't faded, but ever since the squad had talked her into becoming their alternate, she'd discovered that cheerleading could be just as challenging as dance, and that choreographing was almost as exciting as performing.

Almost, but not quite, she thought, as the tape clicked to a stop. Nothing was quite as exciting as performing, not for her, at least. The few times she'd been needed to replace one of the girls on the squad, she knew she belonged in front of an audience. Shy and quiet in "real" life, Melissa onstage was a powerful performing personality.

Unfortunately, being an alternate didn't give her much chance to perform, as her mother had pointed out. Sometimes she couldn't help feeling frustrated. She went to all the practices, worked as hard as anyone, put on her uniform before all the games, and then sat on the sidelines, watching. The times she did get to perform were like a few drops of rain after a long drought — nice, but not enough.

But at least she could choreograph. And next year, when some of the girls would have graduated, she'd have her chance at becoming a regular cheerleader. That will hold you, she thought, tightening the rubber band around her long brown hair and pushing the play button. It'll have to.

As the music started, Melissa raised her arms and drew herself up on her toes, as close as she could get to being *en pointe* in sneakers. With ease, she raised one long leg into the air, but instead of following with a graceful ballet move, she turned slightly and executed a perfect front walkover.

16

"That looks great," Olivia called out from the doorway. "I like it better than what we were doing before."

Flipping her ponytail back over her shoulder, Melissa smiled. "I thought you would. That takes care of that move, then. Just a few more and the cheer should be perfect."

Dropping her canvas bag at her feet, Olivia started doing some leg stretches. "Give me a minute or two and I'll join you."

"Great." Melissa turned off the music and then glanced at the wall clock. "What are you doing here so early?" she asked. "The warm-up's not until half an hour before the game."

"I know." Olivia stopped stretching and sighed. "I needed to escape."

"From what?"

Glancing over her shoulder like a heroine in a horror movie, Olivia whispered, "Boys!" Then she laughed, running her fingers through her brownish-red hair. "Two boys, as a matter of fact."

Melissa laughed, too. "Walt and David, right?"

"Walt and David, David and Walt," Olivia chanted. "I'm going crazy and it's all their fault!" With an exasperated groan, she flopped down on the gym floor, shaking her head and wondering what to do.

Walt Manners, a former cheerleader, had been her first boyfriend, and Olivia thought it would last forever. It didn't. Not that there'd been a major breakup. But Walt had gone off to college in New York, and gradually their relationship had dissolved into friendship.

17

Enter David Duffy, a student at the local college and part-time sports reporter for the *Tarenton Lighter*. He'd started out on the wrong foot with Olivia by writing some stupid drivel about the squad, but it wasn't long before that was behind them, and Duffy, as he preferred to be called, became her new boyfriend.

Re-enter Walt, having left school and having decided to work in Tarenton. Having also decided that he was still in love with Olivia.

Add jealousy from Duffy and what did you get? Two boys competing with each other for the hand of the fair Olivia. It might make a good play, Olivia thought, but this was real life. And real life was beginning to get on her nerves.

"You know the worst part?" she asked Melissa, sitting up and putting her chin in her hands. "They haven't asked me to choose, but I know that's what they expect me to do."

"And you can't decide which one?" Melissa asked.

"No, the worst part is, I don't even know if I want to choose either one of them!"

Melissa thought hard, trying to come up with some advice. But it wasn't easy. She had no idea what it was like to have two boys crazy about her. Actually, it didn't seem like the worst situation in the world to be in, but then, that's not what was bothering Olivia. "If you're not sure how you feel about either of them," she said finally, "maybe you should tell them so. If I were Walt or Duffy, that would scare me so much I'd stop bugging you. For a while, anyway."

"A while," Olivia said, her brown eyes thought-

ful. "That's what I need, some breathing space."
She looked at Melissa and grinned. "And I have
to be honest — I don't want to hurt them, but I
wouldn't mind scaring them off, after all they've
put me through. Does that make me terrible?"

Melissa shook her head. "It makes you just
what you said — honest. And human." She
grinned, too. "Just don't tell them it was my idea."

"Don't worry," Olivia said. "My lips are
sealed."

"I don't want a word out of either of you."
Flattened by the nylon stocking, his lips moved
grotesquely, but his voice was so soft and calm
it reminded Tara of a waiter in an elegant restau-
rant. "What you're going to do, Mrs. Tilford, is
drive out of the garage, turn left, and keep driving
until I give you further instructions." His eyes
shifted to Tara, then back to Mary Ellen. "You'll
stay at the speed limit, you'll keep your eyes on
the road, and you won't do anything unless I tell
you to."

Mrs. Tilford, Tara thought. He knows who
Mary Ellen is. He knows the Tilfords have
money. She looked at Mary Ellen, expecting her
friend to say something, to offer him her purse,
her credit cards, her checkbook. But Mary Ellen
sat like a statue, her blue eyes wide and un-
blinking.

"If it's money," Tara said, her voice hoarse
with fear, "if it's money," she said again, after
clearing her throat, "we'll give you everything we
have. Right here, right now. We don't have to
drive anywhere."

Again, he looked at Tara, and this time the gun followed his gaze. "I thought I said I didn't want a word out of either of you."

Finally, Mary Ellen's eyes moved, and she shot Tara a look of terror and pleading. Please, she seemed to be saying, do what he says.

Staring into the barrel of the gun, Tara took a deep, shaky breath. She was more frightened than she'd ever been in her life. But somewhere, deep inside, she felt something else, something just as strong as fear — anger. This creep had no right to do what he was doing, and the urge to tell him so was so strong she had to grit her teeth to keep from screaming at him. For now, though, for her sake and Mary Ellen's, she'd keep quiet. But she'd keep the anger, too. And if she ever got the chance, she'd use it.

Taking another deep breath — not quite so shaky this time — Tara turned around in her seat.

"Good," he said softly. "I'm glad we got that straightened out. Now, let's drive."

Like a robot, Mary Ellen shifted gears and backed out of the parking space. Only when they'd reached the street did she finally blink — not because the last rays of the setting sun hit her in the eyes, but because everything that was so familiar suddenly seemed alien. It was as though she'd landed in another country, where she didn't speak the language and couldn't read the signs. She must have bought hundreds of hot dogs from that stand on the corner, but now the cheerful man who knew she liked them with ketchup looked like a stranger. She'd waited at that bus stop through snow and rain and ninety-degree temperatures, but now the people standing there seemed like extras in a movie. She'd driven this street almost every day since she got her license, but she couldn't remember if Birch Road had a stop sign or a traffic light.

It had a traffic light, and it turned amber when Mary Ellen was just a car length away.

"Stop," the man ordered, and Mary Ellen did. "Eyes in front," he said. Mary Ellen sensed a movement beside her, and she knew that Tara's green eyes were looking left and right, trying to spot someone they knew.

Why can't she do what he says, Mary Ellen wondered frantically. Doesn't she know what kind of danger we're in? Doesn't she know he's crazy, that he'll probably kill us if we even look at him the wrong way?

As if he could read her thoughts, the man in back chuckled softly. "Glad to see you can follow orders, Mrs. Tilford. It shows you take me seriously. Too bad your friend doesn't. Too bad for your friend, I mean."

Mary Ellen felt Tara stiffen beside her. She wanted to reach out and touch her, for her own comfort as well as Tara's, but she was afraid to move. She was afraid to do anything except what that soft, menacing voice told her to do.

When the light changed, Mary Ellen drove on, through Tarenton's small business district, then past street after street of homes, their porch lights burning brightly in the dusk. Next came a couple of small shopping centers, then some warehouses, and then they were out of town.

21

"Headlights," the man ordered, and Mary Ellen turned them on. "In exactly two miles, you'll come to a road on the right. Turn there."

I know that road, Tara thought. It goes up into the hills. People picnic up there. There probably won't be anybody on it at this time of year because it's not warm enough yet for picnics, and the joggers keep off of it until summer because it's a dirt road. The thought of going there now scared her so much she started to shiver.

Gripping her hands together, Tara ordered herself not to panic. It won't help, she thought, and it might hurt. When we get a chance to escape, I'll never be able to do it if I'm shaking so much I can't run. In spite of her fear, Tara kept telling herself that they'd get out of this. And if they didn't "get" a chance, then they'd make one.

After two miles, Mary Ellen turned onto the dirt road, which climbed bumpily through the low hills on this side of Tarenton. She was almost grateful for the deep ruts and patches of mud. At least they gave her something to concentrate on beside the gun at her head. She was beginning to think they were just going to drive all night, when the voice behind her said, "Okay, stop, right now, and shut off the engine!"

When the car stopped, he told her to turn the headlights on high, and then seconds later, he told her to shut them off completely.

As the darkness closed in, Tara gripped her hands more tightly. "What now?" she asked, trying to keep her voice steady.

As if in answer, she heard a sound in the distance, and as it got closer, she realized it was an engine. Not a car, she thought, maybe a truck. For a moment, she felt a surge of hope. Maybe there *was* someone else on the road, someone who could help them.

But the sound of the engine got louder, then stopped, and suddenly things began to happen very quickly. Tara heard a door slam and footsteps running toward the car. But before she could see who it was, the man in the back pushed her forward roughly, so that her head banged sharply against the dashboard. Beside her, she heard Mary Ellen gasp, and then she was being pulled back up, and a blindfold was tied tightly around her eyes. The driver's door was opened, and she heard someone say, "What happened? Why are there two of them?"

"Just a slight complication," the soft-voiced gunman said. "Don't worry about it. Let's move."

Mary Ellen gasped again, and Tara realized she was being pulled from the car. Then the door on her side was opened, and she felt a hand close tightly around her arm. In a second, she was out, and her hands were tied behind her. She felt a slight push between her shoulder blades and started walking. Off balance, she stumbled and tried to catch herself. But it was impossible, and she fell to the ground. She thought she heard someone sigh, and then a strong hand grabbed her arm. Struggling to stand, she felt her hair catch on something, probably a clump of weeds. "Hey, take it easy!" she cried. "My hair's getting ripped out by the roots!"

Tara didn't expect an apology, and she didn't get one. But she was glad that she'd complained.

She was mad, after all, and as long as she could stay mad, she knew she wasn't completely helpless.

Twenty minutes before he was supposed to be at the gym for the pregame warm-up, Sean Dubrow was driving his red Fiero as fast as the law allowed toward Tarenton. He's just dropped his girlfriend, Kate Harmon, at her house in St. Cloud. They'd spent the afternoon together, first at a sports clinic for little kids where Kate was a volunteer, and then eating hamburgers at a roadside diner between the two towns. A free Saturday afternoon was so unusual for both of them that they hadn't wanted it to end, and they'd sat for a long time in the diner, talking and laughing, not even noticing that the daylight was disappearing outside.

Now Sean had to hurry. But he could make it, he thought, if he got lucky and there weren't any traffic tie-ups. The two-lane highway had been almost empty so far, and he was just about to relax when a dark-colored cargo van pulled out from a side road and started crawling along right in front of him.

The van wasn't really crawling; it was going ten miles under the speed limit, but Sean couldn't help being annoyed, especially since traffic coming the other way started to pick up and he couldn't pull out and pass. He hated getting stuck behind vans like this, the ones that were just high enough to block his view. "987-SLO", its license plate read, and Sean chuckled. Slow fit it perfectly.

When there was no break in traffic after five minutes, Sean politely flicked his headlights up to bright and then back to normal, hoping the driver of the van would take the hint and pull far enough to the right so Sean could get around him. No such luck. He was just about to tap his horn when they hit the Tarenton city limits, where the road had a double yellow line down the middle, which meant he couldn't pass at all anymore. So much for being on time, he thought.

Finally the road widened for a traffic light, and Sean decided to take a detour to the high school. It would cost him a couple of minutes, but since he was already late, two more minutes wouldn't matter. Besides, he didn't want to follow the van any longer than he had to.

Pulling into the left-turn lane, Sean braked for the light and then glanced over at the van. Its driver was staring straight ahead, eyes on the light, both hands tight on the steering wheel. Must be some pretty important cargo, Sean thought.

Then the green arrow flashed on, and Sean made his turn, anxious to get to the high school. Left behind, the van waited, its important cargo tied up in the back, not knowing where they were and wondering in terror what was going to happen to them next.

CHAPTER

In the converted carriage house where Pres and Mary Ellen had lived since they were married, Pres plugged in the vacuum cleaner, turned it on, and began to tackle the thick bedroom rug. The party would take place in the living room and kitchen, of course, so he could have gotten away with a quick straightening up in here. But after what he'd said to Mary Ellen the night before, he thought he owed her something besides an apology, and a completely clean house seemed perfect.

Catching a glimpse of his reflection in the dressing table mirror, Pres crossed his eyes and stuck out his tongue. How could he have picked on her like that? All she'd done was invite a bunch of people over, and he'd reacted like a stuffed shirt because she hadn't consulted him first. When had he gotten to be so starchy, anyway?

Actually, he wasn't starchy at all, and he knew

it. It was just that yesterday had been rough at work, so he'd taken it out on Mary Ellen. It was so easy to do that to someone you were close to, he realized, such an easy trap to fall into.

But not anymore, he thought, grimacing into the mirror again. The next time you've had a rough day at the office, go for a drive, or a run. Or better yet, clean the house.

Pres stuck the hose under the bed and the vacuum cleaner went wild, wailing like a siren. Pulling out the hose, he discovered one of his shoes on the end of it. The vacuum had sucked up the laces and was now trying to finish the rest of it. Pres yanked the shoe off and peered under the bed. Not much dirt that he could see, but plenty of shoes. Mostly his.

Getting down on his knees, Pres started scooping up shoes, pairing them off, and putting them in the closet. He'd left the vacuum cleaner running, so when the phone rang, he didn't hear it.

Mary Ellen handed the phone back and waited, trying not to shake. She stared at her feet, not wanting to look at the two men. Both of them wore the disfiguring nylon stockings over their faces and hats on their heads, and she knew that was so she *could* look at them and never be able to describe them. But she couldn't do it. Even if they ordered her to, she didn't think she could force herself to look them in the eyes, not after what they'd done.

They'd kidnapped her. Her and Tara. They'd brought them to a place she didn't recognize and might never get out of, and now they were waiting for Pres to get home so they could tell him how much money he had to pay to get her back. Pres hadn't answered. But he would, soon. Until then, Mary Ellen looked at her hands, her shoes, the flowered pattern on the rug under her feet, everywhere but at the kidnappers. As long as she didn't look at them, she thought she could keep from screaming.

"Why isn't he there, Mrs. Tilford?" the soft-voiced one asked.

Mary Ellen swallowed. "I don't know. He should be. He will be."

"Twenty minutes," the second kidnapper said, and he took Mary Ellen's arm and led her back to the room where she and Tara were being kept.

It was a small room, with an easy chair, a bed, a footstool, and a table or two. It had a dark brown rug on the floor, a radiator under a nailed-shut window, and peeling, salmon-pink paper on the walls. It was a hideous room, but as the door slammed shut behind her, Mary Ellen actually felt grateful to be back in it.

"They're on the run . . . "
"They're almost done . . . "

In a room just off the gym, four cheerleaders, along with Melissa, chanted softly under their breaths as they went through their warm-up exercises. There was no room here to do a full-fledged routine, but they'd found that saying the words helped put them in the right mood better than just stretching their legs and touching their toes in silence.

"They can't come back," Hope said, puffing a little as she bent at the waist.

Jessica followed with, "The deck is stacked," then came Peter with "The Wolves are here," followed by Olivia's "So let's all hear."

Where Sean's and Tara's lines should have been, there was silence.

"Anybody notice something missing?" Peter asked.

"Two lines," Olivia said. "And two bodies." The two bodies were only five minutes late, so she wasn't really annoyed. "Who wants to guess where they are?"

"Tara's with Patrick," Hope said immediately. "And Sean — "

"Sean *was* with Kate," Peter broke in. Looking at the wall clock, he grinned. "But I'll bet that at this very moment he's dashing madly across the parking lot." Eyes on the clock, he went on in the urgent, excited voice of a sports announcer. "Now he's at the double doors down the hall, but one side is always locked and . . . oh, no! He picked the wrong one! But hang on, folks, it didn't take him long to realize his mistake. Now he's back on track and in the building. He's running, trying to make up for lost time! And he should be crossing the finish line . . ." Turning to the door, Peter held out his arm with a flourish and shouted, "Right now!"

As if on cue, Sean appeared in the doorway, breathing hard, his dark blond hair tousled from his run. "Sorry I'm late," he said. "I got stuck in traffic and then that door down the hall held me up. Why do they always keep one half locked, anyway?"

Everyone laughed as Peter took a bow. "How did you do that?" Jessica asked him in amazement.

"You share a locker room with someone for a year, you get to know their habits," Peter said. "And Sean has a habit of always picking the wrong side of that door."

"Guilty as charged," Sean admitted good-naturedly. Heading for the locker room, he called back, "It'll only take me a couple of minutes to change. That's one of my good habits."

Shaking her head in amusement, Olivia began doing sit-ups. "One body down, one to go."

"Well, Peter," Jessica said, "aren't you going to announce Tara's entrance, too?"

"I'm not sure I could do that twice in a row," Peter said. "And I don't want to ruin a good thing, so I think I'll keep my mouth shut."

True to his word, Sean was back in two minutes and joined the others in limbering up. "Where's Tara?" he asked, suddenly noticing that she wasn't there.

"Nobody knows, not even Peter," Jessica commented wryly, and with another laugh, they all went back to their exercises.

"Are you all right?" Tara asked, staring anxiously at Mary Ellen across the small, dingy room. "What happened?"

Mary Ellen shivered and wrapped her arms around herself. "I'm okay," she said. "They made me call Pres. But he wasn't home."

"Call Pres? What — " Tara had started to ask "what for?" but before the words were out of her mouth, she knew the answer. "Kidnapped? You mean we've been kidnapped?"

Mary Ellen started to nod, then changed her mind and shook her head. "It's me they wanted. You were just . . . there." Her eyes filled with tears. "I'm sorry, Tara."

Tara made a motion as if to brush Mary Ellen's words away and then crossed the room to her side. For a moment they stood together, their arms around each other for comfort. Finally, Tara stood back and glanced around her. "The least they could have done was decorate the room for us. This place is an insult!"

Mary Ellen tried to laugh, but it came out as a gulp. Tara's trying to be strong, she told herself. The least you can do is meet her halfway. Swallowing hard, she tried again and managed a shaky laugh. "They don't have very good taste, do they?"

"They don't have any taste at all," Tara said. Good, she thought. If Mary Ellen had started crying, then I would have, too. Now maybe we can both hang on. "At least we have a bathroom," she said, pointing to a door on the far wall. "But never mind about the decor. Let's start figuring out what we're going to do. I already checked the window. Not only is it nailed shut, but it's got an iron grill on the outside. I guess we couldn't expect them to ignore such an obvious way out."

"Way out?" Mary Ellen stared at her. "What are you talking about?"

"Escape," Tara said. "I mean, it might be impossible, but at least we can try, right?"

Wrong, Mary Ellen thought. Trying to escape would be about the worst thing they could do. What was the matter with Tara, did she want to get them killed? Because that's what would happen, Mary Ellen was sure of it. This was no game, no joke. It was deadly serious.

Tara was walking around the room now, tapping the walls and testing the floor as if she expected to find a hidden panel or a trapdoor.

"Tara, let's just stay calm," Mary Ellen said. "One of those men said they'd try Pres again in twenty minutes. I'm sure he'll be home then. And once they tell him what to do, he'll do it, and we'll be free."

"Fine," Tara said. "But if you want me to stay calm, then I have to do something. I can't just sit here and wait — not even for twenty minutes — or I'll go crazy. Hey!" She stopped moving and actually smiled at Mary Ellen. "That's an idea. I could fake an attack of hysteria. In fact, I probably wouldn't have to fake it. There have to be people around — we're not in the middle of nowhere because I can hear cars driving by. Someone would hear me and maybe call the police."

Just as Mary Ellen was about to protest, Tara went on. "No, I guess it wouldn't work. They'd just put that disgusting gag around my mouth before I got a chance to make much noise."

Tara was serious, Mary Ellen realized. She honestly believed they could get away, like people did in books and the movies. Except this wasn't a movie, this was real. And if they were shot trying to get away, the bullets would be real, too.

Smiling to himself, Patrick climbed out of the small van his company used for light jobs and crossed the parking lot toward the high school gym. He'd just finished overseeing a big move — a household, including a baby grand piano — and he was tired. But the look on Tara's face when she saw him at the game would be worth it.

Joining the crowd of people streaming into the building, he almost laughed out loud. Tara had actually fallen asleep holding the phone last night. He couldn't blame her, really. After all, he'd kept her waiting a long time and it had been late to begin with. But he still couldn't wait to tease her about it. Patrick loved teasing Tara, watching her green eyes flash as she tried to think of something to tease him back with.

He wished he'd had a chance to talk to her today, but when he'd finally gotten a chance to call, she was gone. Wait till she saw him up there in the stands — she wasn't expecting him, and she'd be completely surprised. And not only would he be at the game, he'd be able to go to the party, too. But he'd save that surprise for after he teased her.

As he walked down the hall toward the gym doors, Patrick passed the room where the cheerleaders congregated before a game. He was tempted to stick his head in and say something extremely witty, but then he changed his mind. Sometimes Coach Engborg gave the squad a pep talk before they went out, and he knew she wouldn't appreciate his barging in. Besides, he hadn't thought of anything witty enough yet. He'd do that during the game. Still smiling to himself, Patrick walked into the gym.

It was seven minutes before game time, and in the room that Patrick had just passed, the jokes about why Tara was late had stopped. Olivia had tried to call her house, but the line was busy. Staring at the clock, watching its minute hand make another sweep, she frowned. "I thought she was all past this," she said.

"Past what?" Hope asked.

"Past not being able to do anything except be in love," Jessica answered.

"Right." Olivia started pacing the room, her short red-and-white skirt flipping around her legs. "When Patrick asked her to marry him, that was all she could think of, and she almost got kicked off the squad, remember?"

"But lately she's been great," Hope pointed out. "Always on time, always working as hard as anyone. And being late this once doesn't mean she's going to start doing it all over again."

"Besides, who says she's with Patrick, anyway?" Sean asked with a grin. "Maybe she got stuck behind the same van I did — a real snail."

"I guess it could be something like that," Olivia admitted. "It's just frustrating. And when Coach Engborg finds out, she's not going to be happy at all."

Olivia was right about the coach. Two minutes later, Ardith Engborg stuck her head around the door and asked, "All ready?" Before anyone had

34

a chance to answer, she'd noticed the missing cheerleader. "Where's Tara?"

Olivia cleared her throat. "I don't know, Coach. I tried calling but the line's been busy."

The coach glanced at the clock and pressed her lips into a thin line of disapproval. "Even if she got here now, she wouldn't have time to prepare." She thought for a moment, came to a decision, and nodded her head. "I'll talk to her later. Melissa, you're on. For the whole game."

After she left, Olivia sighed. "See what I mean? Now she's mad. I can't stand it when she's mad, even if it's not at me."

"Well, there's only one way to deal with that," Peter said. "We just go out there and do such a perfect job she'll forget she's mad." He laughed. "Come on, Olivia, it's not that big a deal. Remember, we've got an alternate now, and that's what alternates are for — to be put on the spot. Right, Melissa?"

Melissa smiled and nodded happily. Peter was right, being put on the spot was what she was here for. But the best part was that this was exactly the kind of spot she loved being on.

"Perfect," Pres announced, even though no one was there to hear him. He stuck another chip into the bowl and scooped out some more dip. It was his own recipe, one he'd put together by accident four or five months ago, for another party. Everyone loved it, especially Mary Ellen, who was always asking him what was in it. The key ingredients were sour cream and barbecue sauce, but Pres wouldn't tell her any more than that. He claimed it was a secret, but the main reason he wouldn't tell was because he'd never written it down and had to reinvent it every time he made it.

Swallowing his second bite, he nodded, pleased with himself. He glanced around the kitchen, taking a quick inventory. Cold cuts, cheese, and dip in the refrigerator. Plenty of ice and soda. Popcorn set out by the popper. Napkins, cups, and plates on the counter. Dishwasher empty. Sink scrubbed and floor mopped.

Strolling into the living room, he plumped up a pillow on the couch and put another log in the big stone fireplace. He'd wait an hour or so to light it so it would be just right when the party started.

"Perfect," he said again. Mary Ellen should be home any minute — she'd probably stopped at the library or her family's house — and when she got home, there wouldn't be a single thing for her to do.

The phone rang then, and still feeling pleased, Pres answered it.

When he hung up two minutes later, his handsome face was pale and the satisfied smile was gone. Far from being perfect, his world had suddenly shattered.

CHAPTER

The game was nearing halftime when Pres drove into the Tarenton High parking lot. The Wolves were behind by six points, and even while he was still in the car, he could hear the fans as they shouted along with the cheerleaders in the "Stick With It" cheer.

A couple of years ago, he and Mary Ellen would have been in there, yelling themselves hoarse and trying to do the perfect cartwheel or stag leap. That was before we really knew each other, he thought, before we could even imagine being in love. That was when Mary Ellen used to be ashamed of the little turquoise house her family lived in, when she wanted money more than almost anything. So she went off to New York to become rich and famous. Instead, she grew up, and when she came back to Tarenton she was a very different Mary Ellen Kirkwood, one who'd figured out that money was great, but not the greatest.

Then they'd rediscovered each other, and Pres was finally grateful for the family wealth he'd always taken for granted. He could give Mary Ellen so much, even though he knew she would have loved him even if he hadn't had a dime to his name.

And now this, he thought, opening the car window and letting the cold, late-February air wash over him. All that money that made them so comfortable had turned out to be a ticking time bomb, and when he'd answered the phone almost an hour ago, it had finally exploded.

Not wanting to, but not being able to stop himself, Pres heard once again the smooth, quiet voice on the other end of the line. "Mr. Tilford," it had said, "listen carefully. Are you listening?"

"I'm listening," Pres had said. "Who is this, please?" Still being polite, not knowing what was coming.

"Don't talk, just listen," the voice said. "We have your wife."

The words didn't register for a second, but when they did, Pres had almost laughed. "You what?"

"We have your wife," the voice repeated. "Blonde hair, blue eyes, very pretty. She's wearing blue pants, a white sweater, and a yellow jacket. Knowing you, the sweater's cashmere and the jacket's down. Am I right?"

"What is this?" Pres asked. "Is this a joke?"

There was a short sigh, and then the sound of

a muffled conversation. The next voice Pres heard was Mary Ellen's.

"Pres?"

"Mary Ellen, what . . . ?"

"It's not a joke," she said, and he knew she was terrified. "What he said was true. But I'm all right. Tara and I are all right."

"Tara?"

"Yes. They have us both." Pres heard her take a breath, quick and shaky. "And if you do what they say, they'll let us go."

Before Pres could answer, Mary Ellen was gone and the soft-voiced man was back. "Are you still listening, Mr. Tilford?"

"I'm listening," Pres said again.

"And you're convinced that this isn't a game?"

"I'm convinced."

"And that your wife and her friend haven't been hurt — yet?"

Pres gripped the phone so tightly his knuckles turned white. "Yes!" he said. "Now get to the point and tell me what you want!"

There was a low chuckle. "Oh, I think you can guess what we want, Mr. Tilford."

"Fine, you want money," Pres said impatiently. "How much?"

"Just sit tight, Mr. Tilford. We'll get to that eventually. First things first." Now the voice took on a slight edge. "You tell no one — not your family, not your friends, and especially not the police. I'm sure I don't have to describe what will happen if you go to the police." There was a pause, and then the man said, "Think about it, Mr. Tilford. We'll be in touch."

39

For a full minute, Pres had stood in his picture-perfect living room, listening to the dial tone and trying to convince himself that he was having a bad dream. But then the dial tone turned into a shrill, painful beep that made him slam the phone down and start pacing the room. It was a nightmare, of course. But it was a living nightmare, and it was up to Pres to end it.

If only he'd been able to talk a little longer to Mary Ellen, to hear her say something besides what they'd told her to say. If only they'd told him right then how much money they wanted so he could get it and take it wherever they told him to. If only he could *do* something, right now. But that was part of their strategy, of course. Keep him waiting, let him almost reach the breaking point. Then he'd be so glad to hear from them he'd do anything they wanted, give them any amount of money.

But Pres didn't need to be kept waiting. They didn't need to stretch his nerves because he was already willing to do what they said so they'd free Mary Ellen. And Tara.

The thought of Tara made him stop pacing. He knew her family was fairly well off, but not like the Tilfords. Nobody in Tarenton had the kind of money the Tilfords did, he thought bitterly. Did the kidnappers deliberately take Tara, too, or had she just been unlucky? Would the Armstrongs get a call from the same smooth-voiced man, or was Pres the only one who knew about Tara?

It was then that Pres decided to get in touch with Patrick. He knew he shouldn't, that he was taking a risk, but if he didn't talk to someone, he'd go crazy. Besides, Patrick was his closest friend; Pres owed it to Patrick to tell him.

But it was half an hour before Press could make himself tie up the phone for a quick call to Patrick's office, only to discover that he'd gone to the game. Then it was almost another thirty minutes until he finally left the house. And all the way to the high school, he kept wondering if the phone was ringing, or if someone was following him to make sure he didn't go to the police. Now, in the parking lot, he had to force himself to get out of the car and walk toward the building. Was he being watched?

Shaking off his fear, Pres kept walking. As he got closer, he heard the fans erupt in a loud roar, and he knew Tarenton must have scored. But that was another world, an unreal one compared to the one he was in now.

Just as he got into the hallway, the gym doors opened and the cheerleaders streamed out for the halftime break. "Hey, Pres!" Sean called. "How's it going?"

"We didn't think you'd be here," Olivia said, as Pres joined them. "We thought you'd be getting ready for the party."

The party. Pres had forgotten about it. "It's off," he said bluntly. "I mean, sorry, but Mary Ellen has . . . a cold."

"Oh, that's too bad," Olivia said. "Tell her I'll call her."

"No, don't do that," Pres said quickly. "She's got laryngitis. Can't talk."

"Oh. Well, I hope she feels better." Smiling,

Olivia wiped her forehead and headed for the locker room.

Pres stationed himself by the doors, watching the fans as they poured into the hallway. Finally Patrick emerged, a frown of confusion on his face. "Patrick!"

"Hey, Pres." Patrick lifted a hand and kept on walking. "I'll see you in a second, I just have to — "

"Never mind that," Pres said, taking his arm and steering him down the hall. "I have to talk to you."

"Sure, in a minute, but I want to find out where — "

"I'll tell you." Pres took a deep breath and looked Patrick in the eye. "I'll tell you where Tara is."

"Did you try to give him any hint?" Tara asked. "Some clue or something about where we are?"

Mary Ellen stared at her. "How could I do that? I don't know where we are. Describing this room wouldn't do any good. Besides," she added coolly, "I just couldn't see myself dropping clues when there was a gun pointed at my head."

"I'm sorry," Tara said quickly. "It was a stupid question. Forget I asked it."

In silence, the two girls stared at the plates of untouched food in front of them. Tuna sandwiches on dry white bread, potato chips, and milk. One of the kidnappers — not the one in the car, Mary Ellen noticed, this one was shorter and huskier — had brought it in earlier. Tara

42

asked him what was happening, but he'd ignored her and left without a word, locking the door behind him.

Finally, Tara picked up her sandwich and took a bite. Seeing the look on Mary Ellen's face, she shrugged. "I'm not hungry, believe me," she said. "But not eating will just make us weak. And we need all the strength we can get."

"We'll be out of here before we faint from hunger," Mary Ellen said. "Pres knows now. He'll do what they want, and then it'll be over."

"But we don't know how long that will take," Tara argued. "They're probably asking for a lot of money, and it'll take Pres a while to get it. They probably want unmarked bills, or old bills, or whatever people like that ask for."

"I guess you're right," Mary Ellen said. But she still didn't touch her food.

Tara finished half her sandwich, then looked at the other half. "It tasted like sawdust," she announced, "If I eat any more, I'll be sick." Suddenly, she scooted to the edge of the easy chair, her eyes bright. "You know, that's a tuna fish sandwich. It's got mayonnaise in it. And either the fish or the mayonnaise — or both — could be spoiled. I *could* get sick."

"Then don't eat any more," Mary Ellen suggested.

"No, that's not the point. The point is that if I came down with food poisoning, they'd have to do something," Tara explained. "Call a doctor, or take me to a hospital. Anyway, it's worth a try."

"It is not worth a try," Mary Ellen said tightly.

"Don't you understand? This isn't television. Those men aren't actors. This is for real."

It was Tara's turn to stare. "I know it's for real," she said. "Why do you think I'm trying to find a way out?"

Mary Ellen pulled her jacket around her. She was cold, even though the radiator was hissing. "I think you're being completely unrealistic," she said. "If we want to stay safe, then we should just stay put."

Was she being unrealistic? Tara wasn't sure. Of course, she wasn't planning to hide behind the door and bop the kidnapper over the head when he came to get their plates. That *would* be stupid. Besides, there wasn't anything to bop him with. No lamps, no vases, nothing heavy at all. Even the plates were paper.

But that didn't matter. There had to be other things they could do. She couldn't believe Mary Ellen was so willing to just sit there on the edge of the bed and wait for whatever happened. How did she know they'd live up to their end of whatever bargain they'd made with Pres? After all, they weren't exactly honest, upstanding citizens. Tara wasn't about to trust their word on anything.

Settling back in the chair, Tara drank some more milk and started thinking of ways to escape. She was sure she could. After all, just because the kidnappers had a gun didn't mean they were any smarter than she was. As far as she was concerned, she and Mary Ellen should do everything they could to get out of this dingy little room, and fast.

* * *

It was easy to see Patrick's face in the glare of the school's outside lights, and as Pres told him what had happened, he watched his friend look skeptical, then go pale, and then he saw the anger starting to build.

He feels the same way I do, Pres thought, and even though he hated having to tell such lousy news, he couldn't help feeling grateful that he had someone to share it with, someone who understood completely what he was going through.

Patrick had asked several questions, but now he was silent, his brown eyes dark with a combination of fear and anger.

Anxiously, Pres checked his watch. He'd been gone twenty minutes. What if they'd called? "I've got to get back," he said. "I've been gone too long already. If you want to come and wait with me, that would be great. I sure wouldn't mind the company."

"Wait a second." Patrick shook his head as if to clear it. "I'll come and wait with you, sure. But what about the police? You were the one the kidnapper called — the police will want to know exactly what he said, what his voice was like. I'd go report this, but you're the one they'll want to talk to. Let's go there first. Then we can go to your house and wait."

"Are you kidding?" Pres shook his head, too, in disbelief. "Telling the police is out. I told you what that guy said."

"What did you expect him to say?" Patrick asked. "That's what they always say."

"Sure, because they don't want to get caught." Pres started toward his car. "Well, I'd like to see them caught. But I'm not going to tell the police and let them mess things up."

"Wait a second." Patrick put out his hand and caught Pres's arm. "The police aren't going to mess things up. You've been seeing too many movies about idiot cops."

"I haven't been seeing any movies," Pres told him. "All I know is what that creep told me. And I'm going to do what he said."

"Yeah, but it's not just you anymore," Patrick said. "I'm in this, too. And what about Mary Ellen's family, and Tara's? What are you going to tell them when they start asking questions?"

Pres looked at the dark sky and sighed, his breath frosty in the cold air. "I'll think of something, okay? Anyway, it might be all over before I even have to think of something. Right now I just want to get home." He took a few more steps and then looked back at Patrick, who hadn't moved. "Are you coming?"

Patrick jammed his fists into his pockets. "Sorry," he said. "But if you won't go to the police, then I'll have to."

"I don't believe this!" Pres cried, walking back and facing his friend. "You didn't get that telephone call. I did. You didn't hear that guy threaten Mary Ellen and Tara. I did. You don't know what you're up against."

"You're right," Patrick agreed. "I don't know and neither do you. That's why I'm going to the police."

From the gym came the sound of another happy roar from the crowd, followed by the chanting of the cheerleaders. "Hey, Tarenton, sink it again!"

"I'm going to tell them everything I know," Patrick went on, "but you're the one they'll want to talk to."

"Hey, Tarenton, don't give in!"

"And I'm not going to keep anything back," Patrick said. "So if you go home now, you can expect the police to get there in about an hour. It seems like it would be a lot safer — if anybody's watching your house — to go to the station instead of having a blue-and-white police car pull into your driveway."

"Hey, Tarenton, show 'em how to win!" The crowd in the gym screamed with delight, but neither Pres nor Patrick paid any attention. They stared at each other for what seemed like a long time, and then finally, Pres nodded. But it was a grudging nod, and his eyes were cold.

As the Tarenton Wolves got another basket and the crowd went wild, the two boys walked wordlessly to their cars.

CHAPTER

"Here's to us," Sean said, lifting his Coke glass in the air. "We did a great job tonight — even the coach thought so!"

Hope looked surprised. "She did? I didn't hear her say that."

"She didn't exactly come right out and say it," Sean admitted. "But she didn't say anything bad, either, so I decided to take that as a positive reaction."

The cheerleaders and Kate were squeezed around one of the tables at The Pizza Palace. No one had felt like going home, especially since Tarenton had won with a spectacular shot during the final five seconds of the game. The party at Pres and Mary Ellen's was off, but that was no reason to cancel the celebration.

"Well, if we're going to have a toast, then let's not leave our alternate out of it," Olivia said, smiling at Melissa. "She really came through."

"Right," Peter agreed. "I shudder to think what would have happened without her."

"I can tell you," Jessica said. "Diana Tucker would have made the supreme sacrifice and offered to take Tara's place."

Everyone laughed. Diana, a blonde girl from California, was talented, and her main goal in life was to become a varsity cheerleader. But since she used schemes and tricks to try to reach that goal, she was the squad's least favorite person.

"I think you're right," Olivia told Jessica. "I'm convinced Diana had a uniform made up for herself and she keeps it stashed in her locker so she'll be ready to leap in if the chance ever comes up."

"Well, here's hoping it doesn't," Sean said. "And here's to Melissa, who didn't miss a beat tonight, and here's to us."

Everyone lifted glasses of Coke and Seven-Up, and when the pizza arrived, they dug in hungrily. Even though Melissa usually joined the cheerleaders in their after-game celebrations, tonight she felt more like she belonged. She'd done just what she was supposed to do — filled in — and she'd done it well. It had been great, not having to sit by and watch, and she couldn't help wishing it could happen more often. Lifting a slice of pizza, she asked, "Has anyone found out what happened to Tara?"

Jessica shook her head, her mouth full. Swallowing quickly, she said, "I tried calling right after the game, but the line was busy again."

"That must have been Tara," Sean suggested, his eyes twinkling. "She was probably being grilled by Coach Engborg. Don't bother calling

49

again — if Tara didn't have a good excuse, she'll be tied up all night trying to explain herself."

Just about the time the cheerleaders were working their way through the first of two pizzas, Patrick and Pres were being led down a hallway in the building of the Tarenton Police Department. First they'd spoken to an officer at the front desk, who'd raised his eyebrows skeptically when they said they wanted to report a kidnapping. Patrick could hardly blame him. After all, Tarenton wasn't a big city, it was a fairly peaceful town. Crime wasn't unknown, but it wasn't an everyday occurrence, either — especially something like kidnapping.

Pres was still angry about coming to the police at all, and Patrick had had to do most of the talking. Fortunately, the little Pres did say seemed to have convinced the officer that they were serious, and after waiting about twenty minutes — in silence — they were finally being taken to see an inspector. Patrick just hoped this man wouldn't waste any time thinking they were pulling some kind of prank.

The room they were taken to looked familiar — a lot like the rooms Patrick had seen on television — metal desks, fluorescent lights overhead, Styrofoam cups half filled with coffee, several police officers clacking away at typewriters or chatting to each other. It was quieter than a television show's squad room, though. No one was being led away in handcuffs, no one was rushing to get to the scene of a crime, the phones weren't ringing with calls from hysterical victims. In fact, the phones weren't ringing at all.

Patrick had expected the place to be quiet; what he hadn't expected was that the inspector whose desk they were led to would be a woman. Then he remembered a story in the paper about the first woman inspector in Tarenton. It had been a big deal at the time, but since then he hadn't read anything about her and he'd figured she was probably bored with Tarenton's slow crime scene. Well, she won't be bored anymore, he thought grimly.

The inspector, a tall, slender woman about forty years old, had a strong handshake and a no-nonsense look in her hazel eyes. She introduced herself as Joan Albright, unfolded two metal chairs for Pres and Patrick to sit in, and listened very carefully while Pres told his story.

When he finished, she nodded. "What time did you get the call, Mr. Tilford?"

"I guess it was about seven or seven-thirty," Pres said.

"And you say your wife would have left the mall at four?" Inspector Albright asked.

"That's what time her modeling job ends," Pres said. "I don't know if she left right away. Sometimes she does some shopping afterwards."

The inspector nodded again and turned to Patrick. "What about Miss Armstrong? Did you know what plans she'd made for today?"

Patrick shook his head. "I haven't talked to her since last night," he said, trying to forget how he'd put Tara to sleep with his endless attention to business. "She talked about the party — Pres and Mary Ellen were going to have a party after

51

the game tonight — but she didn't tell me what she was going to do before that. . . ."

The inspector made a note on a yellow pad and said, "We'll be talking with her family, of course. Maybe she told them where she was going."

Pres shifted impatiently in his chair. "I know her family has to be told," he said, "but I don't understand what help they can be. She — and Mary Ellen — were kidnapped. What difference does it make what they were doing?"

"It could make a lot of difference," Inspector Albright told him. "If they were taken from the mall, maybe someone saw it, without even realizing what was happening. Then we'd have a witness, maybe even a description." She made another note. "We'll need pictures of Tara and Mary Ellen," she added. "You wouldn't happen to have snapshots with you, would you?"

Patrick reached for his wallet, where he carried Tara's picture, but Pres didn't budge. "Listen," he said, "I didn't want to come to you in the first place. The only reason I'm here is because Patrick said he'd come even if I didn't." His voice was rising; a couple of police officers turned to look at him, and he took a deep breath. "The idea of you going around showing their pictures to people scares me silly," he went on, more quietly this time. "What if one of the kidnappers hears about it? I mean, I don't know how many of them there are. But the guy said 'we.' That could mean two or twenty, and if you go around splashing their photographs all over the place, one of them might find out. And I don't even want to think about what would happen then!"

In spite of his efforts to control it, Pres's voice had risen again until he was almost shouting. Patrick put a hand on his arm, but Pres ignored him. He was furious at Patrick. How could he be so willing to trust the police? Look what was happening — this inspector was all set to show pictures and ask questions. She might as well take out a full-page newspaper ad, maybe even put up posters and go on television. This whole thing had been a mistake, and Pres was terrified that it would backfire.

Inspector Albright waited quietly, making some notes, until she sensed that Pres had calmed down. Then she said, "I understand your fear, Mr. Tilford. And I don't blame you for it. But, believe me, we aren't going to 'splash' their photographs all over the place. That could be dangerous, I agree."

"I don't see how you can keep what you're doing a secret," Pres argued. "What are you going to do, say you're from a talent agency and you want to hire them, so would somebody please tell you where they are?"

The inspector smiled but shook her head. "I'm not going to go into detail, mainly because I haven't worked it out yet," she said. "I'm afraid you'll just have to trust us."

Her voice was quiet and firm, and Patrick knew she'd said all she was going to say on that subject. Pres could argue all he wanted, but the inspector was calling the shots. Patrick trusted her. He knew he didn't have any choice, anyway, so he was glad he felt like she knew what she was doing.

But Pres was obviously not satisfied, even though he didn't say so. He slumped back in the chair, then sat up straight again, looking at his watch. "I've got to go home," he said, and stood up. "I've been gone over an hour. He might have called."

"I doubt it," Inspector Albright said. "Considering what he told you, I wouldn't be surprised if he waited at least a day. You were probably right about that, Mr. Tilford — he wants to let you sweat awhile."

"Yeah, well, he's getting what he wanted," Pres told her. "But what if he *did* call? What's my excuse for not being there?"

"Tell him you *were* there," the inspector suggested. "That you haven't left your house and the phone hasn't rung at all." She smiled briefly. "Blame it on the phone company."

Pres didn't smile back, but he had to admit it was a good idea. He nodded, then reached for his car keys, anxious to be gone.

But there were more details to settle before he could go back to his empty house. While Pres fidgeted with his keys, Inspector Albright outlined the plan: She and another police officer would soon take up residence with Pres. They'd be tapping his calls and telling him exactly how to respond when the important one finally came. Pres looked even unhappier about this.

"What if someone's watching the house?" he asked. "What are they going to think when two police officers come driving up?"

"We won't advertise the fact that we're police

officers," she explained patiently. "If your house is being watched — and I doubt that it is — whoever's watching it will see a man and a woman arrive. And you'll simply explain that we're relatives. You weren't expecting us, and there's no way you can make us leave."

Pres nodded again. He knew he didn't control the situation anymore, and it made him feel helpless. Helpless to do anything for Mary Ellen but sit back and wait, hoping that this detective knew her job. Because if she didn't, if she blew it, she wouldn't be the one to pay for her mistakes. Mary Ellen and Tara would pay for them.

"Now," the inspector was saying, "about the families. They should be told, of course. Keeping it from them would not only be difficult, it would be unfair."

"I just remembered something," Pres said. "Mary Ellen wouldn't have stopped at her parents' house after leaving the mall. Her family's away for the weekend, visiting an aunt. They left last night." He was relieved. At least he wouldn't have to face Mary Ellen's parents and her little sister, Gemma. Not yet, anyway. "I'll tell *my* parents, tomorrow, I guess. They went to a business party and they won't get home for at least two or three hours. I might as well let them get a good night's sleep." He sighed and rubbed his eyes. "I wouldn't tell them if I didn't have to," he went on. "But it's my father's money that's going to get Mary Ellen and Tara back. When people talk about the 'Tilford millions,' they're talking about Dad's, not mine."

"And how will your parents feel about that?"

Inspector Albright asked. "Believe me, I'll do everything to see that we don't have to touch your father's money," she said, "but just in case we do, I need to know if he'll cooperate."

"Yes, he'll cooperate," Pres said softly. "My parents love Mary Ellen, too."

Finally, the inspector let Pres go, and without exchanging a word with Patrick, he left the room.

Patrick cleared his throat. "I'd like to come with you when you tell the Armstrongs," he said. "If that's okay."

"Of course." Inspector Albright stood up and reached for a tan canvas shoulder bag. "You have your car? Then I'll follow you."

Patrick wasn't sure why he wanted to be there when the Armstrongs found out what had happened to Tara. There was no love lost between them, even though they'd been a lot friendlier since he and Tara had decided against getting married right away. But some day — if things worked out right — he'd be part of their family and thought they deserved to have someone besides a stranger with them when they were told.

He wished Pres had offered to come, too. He couldn't blame him for wanting to get back home, but the Armstrongs were going to have a hundred questions, and Pres was the best one to answer them. But Pres was so angry with him that Patrick hadn't bothered to suggest it.

Thinking of Pres, Patrick couldn't help feeling angry himself. He understood what Pres was going through, but he couldn't believe he hadn't gone straight to the police. Inspector Albright might not be perfect, but she knew this business a lot better than he and Pres did. Patrick was just glad that Pres had decided to tell *him*.

As he drove, Patrick went over the details of his company's next job. Some people were moving to Tarenton and were sending their furniture ahead, to be stored until they found a house. It wasn't a long move — about fifty miles — but it was the first "town-to-town" contract Henley's had landed. Patrick kept his mind on things, like how many boxes they'd need, how long it would take them to pack, reminded himself to get the keys to the storage warehouse — anything to keep from thinking about Tara and Mary Ellen, and what they were going through.

It worked, until he pulled up in front of the Armstrongs' house and saw the porch light glowing warmly in the darkness. He knew it was shining for Tara. But she wouldn't be back tonight, and when he realized that he had no idea when she *would* be back, he felt breathless, as if he'd been punched very hard in the stomach.

Marie, the Armstrong's housekeeper, answered the door, and soon Tara's parents, just back from their dinner party, joined them in the living room. Patrick stood quietly, his hands in his pockets, while Inspector Albright told them what had happened. No one cried or screamed or fainted, but he saw Mrs. Armstrong, an older, auburn-haired version of Tara, reach for her husband's hand and hold it tightly.

When the inspector finished, Marie spoke up. "Tara called about six," she said, in her lilting French accent. "She had been planning to take the bus home from the mall. But it was late, al-

57

most time to go to the school to get ready for cheerleading. So she said Mary Ellen would take her there instead of bringing her home."

"That's good," Inspector Albright said. "At least we know they didn't meet somewhere else, so we can concentrate on the mall."

"Do you think that's where they . . . where it happened?" Mr. Armstrong asked.

"It's hard to say. They could have left and stopped somewhere on the way to the school," the inspector said. "But we'll find out soon."

"Is there anything we should do, anything to help?" Mrs. Armstrong was pale, but she managed to keep her voice from shaking. Patrick knew how hard that must be, and he admired her for it.

"Right now, there's nothing," Inspector Albright said. "But we'll stay in close touch, and if you think of anything that might be helpful, or if you hear anything, contact us right away."

"But what about school and cheerleading?" Mrs. Armstrong said. "People are bound to start asking questions."

"Right," Mr. Armstrong agreed. "We know the importance of keeping this quiet, but what should we say?"

"How about the flu?" the inspector said. "It's still the season for it, and it's the kind of thing that makes you want to stay in bed. That way Tara can be asleep when anyone calls."

After a few more questions and an exchange of phone numbers, Patrick and Inspector Albright were ready to leave. The Armstrongs walked them to the door; Tara's father shook Patrick's hand

and her mother squeezed his arm. Patrick realized that they were trying to comfort him, that they knew he was frightened, too, and he was grateful. He didn't feel quite so alone.

But once he and Inspector Albright had said good-night and driven away in their cars, Patrick felt terribly alone. Even though he knew there was nothing more to say to her, he wished he could have stayed with her longer. She would have been someone to talk to. Mr. and Mrs. Armstrong had each other, Pres didn't want his company, and he had to keep it a secret from everyone else.

By tomorrow, the police would be at Pres's house, monitoring his phone, ready to take action as soon as the right call came in. So, Patrick decided, Pres was going to get his company, whether he wanted it or not. Because Patrick knew he couldn't just sit at home and wait. Something had to happen soon, and he was going to be there when it did.

It was after eleven when the cheerleaders left The Pizza Palace. Melissa was standing in the parking lot, waiting for Jessica, who was going to give her a ride home, when she saw David Duffy drive up.

"Oh, no," Olivia sighed. "It's do-or-die time."

"Do or die?" Sean asked. "That sounds serious."

"It also sounds like it's none of our business," Kate told him.

"Thanks, Kate," Olivia said. "But it isn't any deep, dark secret." She took a deep breath. "I've just got to take the bull by the horns, look him in eye, and let him know what's what."

"Well, that sure makes sense," Sean joked, after Olivia had walked over to Duffy. "Does anybody have any idea what she was talking about?"

Melissa tried not to laugh. Olivia was obviously going to tell Duffy that she didn't want to be pressured anymore, that she wasn't even sure he or Walt were right for her. It *was* serious, but the way she'd put it made it sound funny.

"Like I said, it's not our business," Kate repeated, taking Sean's hand. "Come on, it's freezing out here. I can feel my nose turning red."

Just then Jessica, Hope, and Peter came outside. "I finally got through to the Armstrongs'," Jessica told them. "Now we know why Tara wasn't there — she has the flu."

"So, why didn't she call?" Sean asked.

Jessica shrugged. "Their maid told me it hit real fast and she was on the phone to the doctor most of the night. I didn't actually talk to Tara — she was asleep."

"Now *that* sounds serious,'" Kate said.

"Yeah." Sean agreed. "First Mary Ellen's sick and now Tara." He pretended to shudder and pulled his jacket collar up around his neck. "You don't suppose it's catching, do you?"

"Of course it's catching," Peter said with a grin. "And since you're the one who usually lifts Tara in all the routines, I'd say you're next."

That got a laugh from everybody, and then the cheerleaders headed home, sorry that Tara was sick, confident that she'd be back soon, not worried at all.

CHAPTER

The next morning, as Pres got stiffly up from the armchair and stumbled into the kitchen to make yet another pot of coffee, he decided that nothing was worse than waiting for the phone to ring. He ought to know, he thought. He'd spent a sleepless night doing just that — staring at a piece of electronics covered in beige plastic and willing it, begging it, to ring. But it had stayed silent. Ten times he'd lifted the receiver just to make sure it was still working, and each time he did, he worried that someone had called and gotten a busy signal. There really *were* worse things, he knew that. But for him, this was the perfect torture.

When the coffee was finished brewing, he poured himself a cup and drank some. His stomach immediately protested such terrible treatment. Rummaging in the refrigerator, he pulled out some ham and cheese that he'd sliced for the party, slapped it between two pieces of bread, and ate automatically, not tasting a thing.

The silence in the house was beginning to drive him crazy. It wouldn't hurt to play some music, as long as he kept it quiet. He slipped a tape into the machine, but turned the volume so low that he heard only bits and pieces of sound. That was worse than silence, so he shut the recorder off.

He still had to tell his parents, but he was afraid to use the phone and afraid to leave the house. A shower would have felt great, but he didn't dare take one.

That brought him back to where he'd started — waiting for the phone to ring. He was trying to decide between sitting on the couch or the chair when the sound of the doorbell shattered the silence as well as his nerves, and he almost dropped his half-eaten sandwich.

Peering through one of the small windows on the side of the front door, Pres saw Inspector Albright and a man standing outside. Both were dressed casually, in sweatpants and warm jackets, and both had large canvas carryalls slung over their shoulders.

My unexpected relatives, Pres thought with a sigh. He had to admit they didn't look like the police, but he still didn't want them in his house.

"Morning," Inspector Albright said when Pres opened the door. " No word yet?"

"Nothing," Pres told her and stepped back to let them inside.

"This is Sergeant Michael Wells," she said, waving her hand at the man behind her. He was a little younger than she was, Pres thought. Short and balding, with black eyes that didn't miss a thing. Pres nodded to him, then reluctantly led them both into the living room.

"One or both of us will be here all the time," Inspector Albright said, as they began unloading their canvas bags. "But we'll try to stay out of your way as much as possible." As she talked, Pres watched them pull out two telephones, wiring, and recording equipment, among other things, plus extra sweatshirts and pants, a bag of doughnuts, a can of coffee, and an electric coffee pot. "We both drink too much of this stuff," she explained with a smile. "So we thought we ought to bring our own. If you wouldn't mind showing him where the kitchen is, Mike will get some perking."

"I just made a pot. You can have some of that first." Pres made the offer without much graciousness, but the police officers didn't seem to notice. They thanked him, got themselves some coffee, and went on about their business.

While they were setting up their equipment, they talked quietly to each other about their families — both had two kids — and about the weather, a retirement party for someone on the force, and which team would win the national basketball championship. They were so calm and casual that Pres found himself getting more and more irritated. How could they come into his house and discuss their jobs and their kids while Mary Ellen was being held by some creeps, probably at gunpoint? The least they could do, he thought, is pretend to be worried, even if they weren't.

Finally, Inspector Albright stopped puttering with the extra phones and looked at Pres. "There are a couple of things you should do when you get the call," she said. "You've probably already thought of them, but just in case you haven't, the first is — keep whoever calls talking as long as you can."

"You're going to try to trace the call, right?" Pres asked.

She nodded. "If you went outside, you'd see a telephone company truck and two workmen on the pole right now."

Great, Pres thought sarcastically. They might as well advertise what they're doing.

As if she'd read his thoughts, the inspector smiled. "They're down the road, not right in front of your house," she said. "Fortunately, your line can be tapped there, too. The second thing to do," she went on, "is to insist that you talk to Mary Ellen again. And Tara. The kidnappers may just try to tell you they're all right. Don't let them do that. You want to hear the girls' voices."

Pres couldn't argue with that. More than anything in the world, he wanted to hear Mary Ellen's voice again.

Soon, the two police officers were set up. They offered Pres a doughnut, which he refused; each of them took one, sat down, and began reading the newspaper they'd brought with them. Pres wandered back into the kitchen, wanting to be alone. Over the stove was a ceramic clock painted like a cat's face, and he sat at the table, watching the minutes go by. Once more, there was nothing to do but wait for the phone to ring.

"Well, at least we know now," Olivia said as she hung up the phone in her kitchen.

"Know what?" her mother asked.

"What happened to Tara last night. She has the flu. Their maid sounded worried — Tara must be pretty sick."

"That's too bad," Mrs. Evans said. "I just hope she stays home until she's completely over it. All we need is to have you catch the flu."

Olivia ignored the comment, smiling to herself. It had been many years since she'd been a sickly little girl, but as far as her mother was concerned, it was only yesterday.

The doorbell rang then, and to escape any more remarks about her "delicate" health, Olivia rushed to answer it. When she saw who it was, she was almost sorry she'd hurried.

"It's a perfect day," Walt Manners announced, as soon as she'd opened the door. A tall, husky young man with a friendly, open face, he grinned and pointed to the sky. "Except for a few clouds, of course," he went on, "but they don't count. They're definitely the nonthreatening type. Everyone should be out enjoying it."

Olivia stepped out onto the porch. It was mostly sunny, but the wind was chilly, and she crossed her arms to keep warm. "I'm sorry, Walt," she said. "But I think I'll pass."

Some of the sparkle left his brown eyes. "Got something else lined up? With Duffy, maybe?"

"No, not with him. Not with anyone, in fact." Walt started to say something, but Olivia held up her hand. "Listen," she said. "This is going to sound like a line from a movie, I know, but it's exactly what I want to say — I think it would be better if we didn't see each other for a while."

Walt stared at her skeptically. "It *is* Duffy, isn't it?"

Olivia shook her head. "It's both of you," she said. "I told Duffy the same thing last night."

"You mean . . . there's *someone else?*" Walt put his hand on his heart in a dramatic pose, but Olivia knew him well enough to know he wasn't really joking.

"No, there isn't anyone else." Olivia took a deep breath. "You two have been playing games, trying to 'win' with me for a long time, and it's beginning to bug me. A lot. I want you both to just . . . back off for a while. Because if you want the truth, I'm not sure how I feel about either one of you anymore."

There was no question about it — Olivia meant what she said. And Walt was smart enough to know that if he didn't back off, he'd lose her for sure. That scared him, badly. But to cover his feelings, he gave her another grin, not quite so broad this time, and a little lopsided. "Well, then, I guess enjoying your company is out for a while, huh?"

Olivia nodded. Duffy had reacted differently than Walt; he'd gotten very quiet, but she knew both of them were upset. She'd told Melissa that she wouldn't mind scaring them off, and she didn't. Still, she cared about them, so it wasn't turning out to be fun at all.

"Well, then," Walt said again, "I'll . . . ah . . . I'll just take my leave and let you get on with . . .

66

whatever." Bending forward, he kissed her quickly on the cheek, then trotted down the sidewalk to his car.

Olivia watched him go. That's that, she thought with a sigh, and went back inside. Now what? She'd wanted peace of mind and freedom to think, and now she had it. Except she didn't feel much like thinking at the moment. She felt like doing something.

Suddenly she thought of Melissa. If Tara was so sick she was sleeping in the middle of the day, then it would probably be at least a week until she was back on the squad. Now, not only would Melissa be working on the new cheer, but she'd probably want to practice some of the old ones, just to make sure she had them right. She'd want to make the most of her chance to cheer full-time.

Ten minutes later, Olivia was on her way to meet Melissa at the gym. She'd gone from two boyfriends to none at all, but since she still had cheerleading, it didn't matter. As long as she had splits and walkovers and cartwheels to practice, she'd be fine.

The minute Pres opened the door to him, Patrick could tell he was even more upset than he had been the night before. "What is it?" he asked quickly, frightened by the look on his friend's face. "Has something happened?"

"If you mean did I get another phone call, then no, nothing's happened," Pres said coldly.

Without waiting to be asked, Patrick stepped inside. "Then what is it?" he asked again. "I can tell something new is wrong."

Wordlessly, Pres led him into the living room, where Inspector Albright and another man were sitting. The inspector said hello and introduced Sergeant Wells, while Pres stood by silently. Still not talking, Pres walked into the kitchen and Patrick followed. There was a lot of tension in the air, he thought, and it wasn't just because of the kidnapping.

"It's your two friends out here," Pres said, shutting the kitchen door. "First they come and set up shop in my house and now — " he broke off and shook his head in disgust.

"Now what?" Patrick asked, deciding to ignore the comment about his "two friends."

"Now they say that when I get the call, no matter what the guy says, no matter how much money he asked for, I'm supposed to tell him I need time," Pres told him.

"So? They're probably going to ask for a bundle; most people would need time to get it," Patrick said.

"Patrick, I have a bundle," Pres said, as if he were explaining something very simple to someone not too bright. "My father and I can probably get our hands on just about any amount they ask for. Why do you think they grabbed Mary Ellen in the first place?" He stopped and poured himself a glass of water, thinking about his father, who had dropped by an hour before. It hadn't been easy to tell him what had happened, and his father had been more shaken than Pres had ever seen him. But he'd told Pres that no matter what the kidnappers asked for, he'd get it. "So why should I ask for time?" Pres went on, setting his glass down with a snap. "I don't need time. I need Mary Ellen back. Just like you need Tara."

Patrick nodded. "It still makes sense, though," he said. "I mean, more time for you means more time for the police."

"I don't care about the police," Pres said. "You might, but I don't. Unless they mess things up, of course. Then I'll care about them very much."

Patrick gritted his teeth to keep from arguing. Pres was worn out and strung out; arguing wouldn't do any good. Without saying anything, he pulled out a chair, sat down at the table, and took a paperback book from his pocket.

"What are you doing?" Pres asked.

"Waiting," Patrick said, opening the book. "Just like you."

Later that day, while Pres and Patrick waited in tense silence, and Olivia and Melissa worked out until they were pleasantly exhausted, Sean and Kate were picking their way through half-frozen mud in the hills outside of Tarenton.

"This is not a day for a hike," Sean complained jokingly, as he slid three feet down a small slope. "Why did I let you talk me into it?"

"You said you wanted action," Kate reminded him. "And I wanted fresh air, so this is what we agreed on."

"True, I did want action," Sean said. "But slogging around in mud and weeds wasn't exactly what I had in mind."

Kate laughed. "These aren't weeds," she said. "They're wild blackberry bushes. A few more months and we'll be able to pick them."

"I've got an idea," Sean told her, disentangling his sleeve from one of the bushes. "Let's get out of here and spend those months someplace warm and dry."

"Okay, okay." Kate laughed again. "I'm getting tired, too."

"Tired? I'm not tired," Sean protested. "I could go forever if part of this hill hadn't decided to slide into my boots."

"What's that?" Kate wiped her misty glasses and pointed across the dirt road they were heading for. "Is that a car?"

Sean stopped and looked. "Yes," he said. "It's a car. Unfortunately, since we drove in on another road, it's not my car."

Since they were going in that direction anyway, the two of them made their way down the slope and across the road to the car.

"It looks like it was pushed off to the side into these bushes," Kate said, pointing to the tracks. "It must have broken down."

"Wait a second." Sean looked more closely at the car, a silver-gray compact with an orange pinstripe on the sides. "This looks like Mary Ellen's car."

"Hey, look what I found," Kate called. Bending over a blackberry bush, she pulled out something small and glittering. "A hairclip."

"Umm." Sean was walking around the car, testing the doors. They were all locked. It sure looked like Mary Ellen's car, but unless he got inside and checked the registration — if it was there — he couldn't be sure.

"Shaped like a butterfly," Kate was saying. "Rhinestones and beads. It's really pretty."

But what would Mary Ellen's car be doing out here in the hills? Sean wondered. In fact, what would Mary Ellen be doing out here in the hills? Maybe she and Press had gone hiking, too. Maybe, he thought with a chuckle, that's how she caught her cold.

"It looks brand-new," Kate said, coming over to Sean. "I guess I shouldn't take it."

"What?" Sean was looking at the license plate, but he'd never noticed what Mary Ellen's number was, so he didn't know if this was hers. "Why shouldn't you take it?" he asked, looking at the hairclip for the first time. "I don't think whoever lost it is going to comb the hills for it."

"You're probably right." Kate put the clip in her pocket. "Well, I'll take it with me, anyway. And if I don't hear anybody asking about a lost hairclip, then maybe I'll keep it."

No, Sean finally decided. It probably wasn't Mary Ellen's car. After all, there had to be hundreds of cars like this. "Come on," he said, holding out his hand to Kate. "Let's get back to civilization."

But as they walked away, he couldn't help looking back. There probably *were* a lot of silver-gray cars around, even in a place as small as Tarenton. But with a classy orange pinstripe? He wasn't so sure about that.

CHAPTER

"I don't understand what's happening!" Tara cried. "There's only one reason for kidnapping somebody and that's money. So why don't they hurry up and ask for it and get it over with? What are they waiting for?"

"They probably want to get Pres so worried that he'll actually be glad to hear from them," Mary Ellen said quietly. "And he won't argue about how much they ask for."

It was Monday morning, so early that the sky — what the two girls could see of it through the window grill — looked like pale gray paper, only a shade lighter than it was an hour before. They'd spent a miserable Sunday without any contact with their kidnappers except the one who brought their food and took away the leftovers. And he was about as communicative as a rock, Tara thought. His only comment had been, "Still no appetite?"

"But Pres wouldn't argue anyway," she said.

"I know." Mary Ellen sat on the bed and scooted across it until her back was against the wall. "I guess they *don't* know."

"Just as I thought," Tara commented. "They didn't do their research and they're not very bright." She smiled at her feeble joke, hoping that Mary Ellen would smile back. She didn't. She wasn't grim, though; she was really pretty calm. Calm and patient, Tara thought, willing to let other people take charge of her life.

Tara admired her friend's control, but she still didn't think patient acceptance was the right attitude to have, not in a situation like this. When something like this happened, you owed it to yourself to stay mad and to do everything you could to put yourself in charge.

But how? Tara had spent most of the day and night trying to think of some way to take charge, and she still hadn't come up with anything. The window had a grill and looked out onto a brick wall. The door was locked, and even though the man who brought their food wasn't any taller than she was, she wasn't about to get into a battle with him.

Tara turned sideways in the easy chair and hung her legs over the arm, trying to get comfortable. She felt rumpled and grubby and wished she could shower and change her clothes. But taking a shower would seem like she was making herself at home, and the clothes she'd bought for the party were still in the trunk of Mary Ellen's car, not that she'd wear them in this place. Reaching up to scratch her head, she discovered that one of her new hairclips was missing. It must have been pulled out by those weeds she fell into.

Thinking of the new clothes and the hairclip made her think of Patrick. So far, she'd managed not to. By concentrating on how to escape, she'd kept everything else out of her mind — her parents, Marie, the other cheerleaders, and Patrick. But now she saw his rugged, handsome face so clearly it was as if he was standing right there in front of her.

Quickly, she jumped out of the chair and ran into the bathroom, where she grabbed the thin cotton towel and tried to wipe the tears away before they had a chance to roll down her cheeks.

"Tara?" Mary Ellen was standing in the doorway, looking worried. "Can I help?"

Tara shook her head. "I was just thinking of Patrick," she gulped. Turning on the faucet, she splashed her eyes. "I mean, if I'd known what was going to happen, I wouldn't have fallen asleep while he was talking to me Friday night."

Mary Ellen nodded, smiling a little. "I know what you mean," she said. "Pres and I were in the middle of a really dumb argument when it happened."

Tara looked sympathetic. "And you feel rotten about it, don't you?"

"Yes. I've been promising myself that when this is all over, I'll never argue with him again."

"And I've decided never to talk to Patrick when he's working," Tara said firmly. Then she looked at Mary Ellen and almost laughed. "Who are we kidding? We'll never be able to keep those promises."

"Probably not. But we can try." Mary Ellen smiled again, and for a moment, the two girls felt much better.

"Well," Tara said, dampening the towel and pressing it to her eyes. "At least I didn't cry too much. Maybe my eyes won't get all puffed up the way they usually do. I don't know when our 'waiter' will be back, but the last thing I want is for him to see me all blubbery and — " Suddenly, she stopped.

"What is it?" Mary Ellen asked. "You look like a lightbulb just went on in your head."

"It just did," Tara said excitedly. "Listen, you know when there's been a hijacking, the newspapers always runs those stories about the mental state of the prisoners?"

"Yes, and now I know exactly what they're talkng about," Mary Ellen said.

"No, I mean the part about how after a while, the prisoners start to identify with the hijackers," Tara said. "You know, they start to feel like they're on the same side. Maybe that could work for us."

"Somehow, I don't think these two men would believe me if I suddenly said they should take Pres for every penny he's got," Mary Ellen told her. "They've already seen how scared and miserable I am."

"Sure, but what about me?" Tara asked. "They don't know my situation at all. For all they know I could hate Pres, and you, too. See," she went on, "if I made them think I'm on their side, they might start to like me. And then they might start to feel bad about what they've done and let us go."

Shaking her head, Mary Ellen turned and walked back into the bedroom. "Well, why not?" Tara asked, following her. "You have to admit, it's not like some of my other ideas. It's much more subtle. And even if it doesn't work, it won't hurt to try."

"How do you know that?" Mary Ellen stood at the window, staring at the brick wall. "They've probably read the same stories. They'd know what you're trying to do, and instead of feeling sorry for us, they'd get mad. And who knows what they'd do then?"

The friendly, comfortable feeling they'd shared just a minute before was gone. Like Pres and Patrick, they were both in the same boat, but it seemed they were paddling in opposite directions.

"I don't understand you!" Tara burst out in frustration. "How can you sit around and wait for things to happen?"

"I told you. Because it's the safest thing to do!" Mary Ellen turned from the window, her blue eyes flashing. "You think this is some kind of game, or a play you can act your way out of. But it's not, and I wish you'd stop!"

"I do not think it's a — " Tara broke off as she heard the key in the lock. Both girls watched as the door opened, and their 'waiter,' as Tara called him, stuck his head inside. With a flick of his hand, he motioned for Mary Ellen to follow him out of the room.

*　*　*

76

Pres was sure that Saturday night had been the longest night of his life. But then Sunday went by, with no word from anyone except an encyclopedia salesman, a woman wanting to speak to John, and a man asking for Susan. Patrick had gone home late Sunday night, promising to come back some time Monday morning. Pres was still angry with him for dragging the police into his life, but now that Monday had arrived, he found himself wishing that Patrick would hurry up and get here. At least he'd have somebody to share his frustration with.

"It doesn't make sense," he muttered, pacing around the living room. "If they wanted to make me sweat, they've done their job. Why don't they get on with what they really want and call about the money? They're crazy to let all this time go by — something must be wrong."

Sergeant Wells, leaving to check on the investigation at the mall, gave him a sympathetic glance, and Inspector Albright looked up from the crossword puzzle she was working on. "Don't try to second-guess them," she said. "You'll just make yourself more miserable. They've got a lot on their minds, too. When they're ready to call, they will."

She spoke calmly, as usual, and then went back to her crossword puzzle. Pres watched her for a minute. Since she and the sergeant had arrived, they'd kept to themselves as much as possible, talking to him if they had a question, but otherwise waiting until he spoke to them first. They accepted his coffee but brought their own food and entertained themselves by reading books, magazines, and newspapers. Pres knew they were trying their best to stay out of his way and let him be alone, since he'd made it clear that that was what he wanted. But he still resented them.

It's a job to them, he thought, staring out the window at the gray morning sky. And when it's over — no matter what happens — they'll go home, get some sleep, and go back to work at another job. They weren't involved, he thought, so how could they care? And if they didn't care as much as he did, how could he trust them?

How long had he been looking out the window? Pres's eyes focused and he realized that Sergeant Wells was driving up. Pres hurried to open the front door, anxious to know if he'd learned anything.

The sergeant shook his head at the questioning look on Pres's face. "Sorry," he said, as they moved into the living room. "Plenty of people saw the two girls together, but no one saw them with anybody else. We've got a witness who thinks she saw a car fitting the description of Mrs. Tilford's heading west once it left the parking garage, but she's not completely sure."

Even though Pres had been against questioning people at the mall, he couldn't help feeling a tremendous letdown, and Inspector Albright noticed. "They just got started," she said gently. "They'll keep trying all day, so try not to feel too disappointed yet."

Pres nodded, not looking at her. He didn't want sympathy, he wanted action.

Instead of action, though, the two police officers settled down in their chairs and began going over some paperwork together. They both looked so relaxed that Pres felt an almost overwhelming urge to tear the papers out of their hands and remind them that this wasn't an office, it was his home. And the reason they were in his home was because his wife had been kidnapped.

Biting his lips to keep from giving in to the urge, he wheeled around and headed for the kitchen. When he was almost to the door, the phone rang.

Pres had wanted action, and he got it now. In a second, the two officers were at their phones, and the sergeant had pressed a button on his tape recorder.

His heart jumping wildly in his chest, Pres walked quickly back into the room and put his hand on the telephone. "On three," Inspector Albright said and began counting.

Simultaneously, the three receivers were lifted, and simultantously, they all heard the distinctive soft voice that had changed Pres's world.

"Mr. Tilford?"

"Yes?"

"Have you been thinking about what I said during our last conversation?"

"Yes." Then, as his eyes met Inspector Albright's, Pres said, "I want to talk to Mary Ellen."

"Of course."

Another second, and Mary Ellen came on. "Pres, I . . ."

"Mary Ellen, are you all right?"

"Yes, I'm fine," she said. She spoke softly and she sounded scared, but as far as Pres could tell, she was as fine as anyone could be in such a situation. "Tara and I are both still okay."

"Mary Ellen, I . . ." Pres started, but once again, the kidnapper had taken back the phone.

"Now, then, Mr. Tilford," he said. "Are you ready to talk business?"

Pres was ready, but Inspector Albright wasn't. Her hazel eyes insisted that he do what she'd told him. Gripping the phone, Pres said, "I want to talk to Tara first."

"You mean you don't believe your wife?" The kidnapper sounded shocked. "She said her friend was fine."

"I still want to talk to her." Pres gritted his teeth and went on. "I won't do anything until I talk to Tara."

"I'm sorry to hear that, Mr. Tilford," the man said. "But I'm sure you'll change your mind."

"Why can't you just put her — " Pres stopped, staring at the phone in disbelief. The dial tone was back; the kidnapper had hung up.

Looking across the room, he saw that the two police officers had already hung up. The sergeant was using his phone to make a call, and Inspector Albright was standing in front of the tape recorder, watching it intently as it rewound.

Suddenly, all of Pres's fear and frustration rose to the surface. "I can't believe this!" he burst out. "That guy was just about ready to ask me for the money. And if I hadn't told him I wanted to talk to Tara, I might be that much closer to my wife *and* to Tara right now."

Inspector Albright started to answer, but Sergeant Wells spoke first. "They couldn't trace it," he said, hanging up his phone. "Not enough time."

"No, I didn't think there was, " the inspector said. She glanced at Pres. "It wasn't your fault, Mr. Tilford."

"I know it wasn't my fault," Pres said coldly. "I did what you told me to do. But if I'd had my way, I'd still be on the phone right now, talking money. And then you might have had enough time to trace it, did you ever think of that?"

Inspector Albright shook her head. "It wouldn't have happened that way, believe me. Unless that man's a total fool — which I doubt — he's not taking any chances on long telephone calls. He might think he scared you enough to keep you away from the police, but he can never be sure."

Pres shut his eyes briefly and took a deep breath. "I shouldn't have asked to talk to Tara," he said, trying to keep his voice under control. "Mary Ellen said they were both okay, and I could tell she wasn't lying."

"You're probably right," the inspector agreed. "But by demanding to talk to Tara, you let the kidnappers know that they can push you just so far. You'll give them money — you're not arguing about that — but you have to know that both girls are all right before you do. And you have to hear them both say it." She rubbed her eyes, which were shadowed underneath from lack of sleep. "If they thought you were a total pushover, they'd probably ask for one amount of money and then raise the price at the last minute. Or, in a few months, or even a year or two, they just might decide to come back for seconds. Did you ever think of *that?*"

She spoke quietly, as usual, but she sounded tired, and Pres heard a note of disappointment in her voice. Maybe she does care, a little, he admitted to himself. And as for what she'd just said, well, he *hadn't* thought about it. He was just about to reply when the phone rang again, and the tension immediately came back into the room.

Again, the three of them took their places, but when Pres answered the phone, someone asked to speak to Sergeant Wells. The other two hung up while he took the call.

"Right," he said. "Yeah, okay. Good, thanks." The sergeant put the phone down and smiled at Pres and Inspector Albright. "A break," he said. "It was a local call."

"Local?" Pres frowned. "You mean it was made from right around here?"

"Not 'around,' " Inspector Albright said, the tiredness gone from her voice. "It was made from right here in Tarenton. Mary Ellen and Tara are being held somewhere in this town."

CHAPTER

"I think it's just about there." Melissa bent from the waist and took a couple of deep breaths. Straightening up, she looked at the rest of the cheerleaders. "Can we try it one more time?"

"Oh, no, a pun!" Peter faked a groan.

It was late Monday afternoon, and the squad had been working on the revised version of the "One More Time" cheer for almost an hour. Melissa's new steps weren't easy, and even though everyone was getting tired, they knew the cheer was going to be a knockout.

Melissa laughed at Peter's remark. "I guess it was a pun, but I didn't mean it to be."

"Well, in that case, I suppose we could manage to do it again," Sean joked.

"Sure we can," Olivia said. "It's looking great, and besides, Coach Engborg's going to be here in about fifteen minutes. Let's really surprise her!"

Quickly, the cheerleaders got in position, Melissa and Jeessica off to the sides, Hope and Olivia in the middle, paired with Sean and Peter. At the count of three, they began, starting off gracefully with some back and front walkovers that appeared to be done in slow motion. Gradually, the cheer picked up speed, and the movement did, too. From slow walkovers, the squad went into a dance step that got faster and faster. Then they broke from the dance, spread themselves out, and ended with a series of cartwheels and forward flips performed so quickly that the cheerleaders were nothing but a colorful blur of motion.

They held their final pose for a few seconds, then collapsed to the floor, breathless and laughing. "I hope that looked as good as it felt," Jessica commented, stretching out on her back.

"It did, I could tell," Sean said. "In fact, I'd say it was just about perfect, and I guarantee it'll knock the coach's socks off."

"Well, I still have my socks," Ardith Engborg's voice rang out. She was standing at the side doors, a smile tugging at the corners of her mouth. "But I must admit, they need pulling up." Striding across the shiny floor to the group of cheerleaders, she said, "That didn't look bad at all. I didn't expect to see any changes so soon."

"It's all because of Melissa," Hope told her. "I think she's been working on it twenty-four hours a day."

"Right," Peter agreed. "We came in here expecting a regular workout, but Melissa had other ideas."

"You can't blame just me," Melissa said with a laugh, enjoying their friendly grumbling. "Olivia worked on it with me yesterday."

"I knew it!" Sean snapped his fingers. "A conspiracy!"

"Whatever it was, it worked," the coach said. Her smile got a little bigger. "And now that you've done such a good job on that cheer, what do you say we work on a couple of others?"

There was more good-natured grumbling as the cheerleaders picked themselves up off the floor, but for another half hour, they worked hard and willingly, enjoying the teamwork that made their routines so special.

Watching them, Coach Engborg was pleased again that she'd decided to add an alternate to the squad. Look at the way Melissa stepped right into Tara's place, with almost no hitches. Not that she was like Tara at all — Tara was a bundle of energy, whirling around the gym like a blazing light, while Melissa was smooth, graceful, and refined. But she fit in beautifully, and as long as she did that, the coach was satisfied.

"All right," she called, when the workout was over. "That was pretty good. The game's at Garrison tomorrow after school, so don't forget and take off the minute the bell rings. See you in the parking lot, three o'clock sharp."

"*Pretty* good?" Sean said when she'd left. "I thought we rated at least a good."

"Don't worry, we did," Olivia assured him as they all headed for the locker rooms. "I could tell she liked what she saw. Let's just make sure she likes what she sees tomorrow, too."

"I wonder if Tara will be back tomorrow," Hope said.

Jessica shook her head. "I called her at lunch today, and she's still sick."

"How did she sound?" Peter asked.

"I don't know, I didn't talk to her," Jessica said. "She was asleep. Marie told me she still wasn't feeling well."

"Well, even if she did come back tomorrow, she wouldn't be ready for 'One More Time,'" Olivia said. "She doesn't know the new steps yet. I guess we'll have to have an extra practice when she gets rid of whatever bug she's got."

Melissa had been holding her breath ever since Hope had asked about Tara. Now she let it out, hoping no one noticed how relieved she felt. Of course, it was too bad that Tara was sick, but as long as she was, Melissa was just as glad she wouldn't be recovered by tomorrow. At least I'll have a chance to cheer at a game, she thought, and so, as ignorant as everyone else about what was really "wrong" with Tara, she went happily into the girls' locker room.

In the boys' locker room, Sean showered and changed quickly, eager to get out to Kate's house and take her for a quick Coke before they both had to go home and study. But when he got onto the stretch of highway between Tarenton and St. Cloud, he remembered the car he and Kate had found the day before, and to satisfy his curiosity, he turned onto the road leading into the hills. He was sure the car wouldn't be there today, so he was surprised when he saw it, still sitting in a tangle of blackberry bushes.

It couldn't be Mary Ellen's car, he told himself again. If it was, she and Pres would have moved it by now. Unless it had been stolen and they didn't know where it was. He backed his own car up until the road widened enough for him to turn around, then glanced in his rearview mirror. It sure looks like her car, though, he thought. Maybe he'd give Mary Ellen a call, just to find out.

Patrick had come back to Pres's house after lunchtime, and now he was in the kitchen again, watching Pres stare at the refrigerator, as if it might be able to tell him where Mary Ellen was.

Patrick had gone through the morning like a robot, making arrangements with the storage warehouse, getting boxes, giving instructions to his crew. Since it was their first "long distance" move, he wouldn't have missed it if things had been normal. But things weren't normal. His crew had been surprised he wasn't going to be with them, and Patrick couldn't blame them, but he knew he couldn't go. He had to be here, at Pres's, until . . . until something happened.

"What do you think they'll do now?" he asked.

Pres dragged his eyes from the two banana-shaped magnets on the refrigerator door. "What do you mean?"

"I mean, now that the police know Tara and Mary Ellen are being held here in Tarenton," Patrick explained. "I guess they'll start some kind of search. Have they said anything?"

Pres nodded. "They thought it was good news about them being in here," he said. "They said it narrowed it down, made it easier to look, ask questions, find out if anyone noticed anything unusual in their neighborhood." Reaching out, he pulled the magnets off the door and clicked them together in his hands. "Or course," he added, "if they'd just let me handle the call the way I wanted to, they wouldn't have to search around and ask questions. Mary Ellen and Tara could have been back by now."

Patrick didn't say anything, but he wasn't as sure about that as Pres was. He didn't blame Pres for being frustrated, but it seemed like Inspector Albright was making sense about not being a pushover. And she couldn't have just made it up, she'd been trained to handle things like this. Patrick was scared, but he was still willing to trust her. He wished Pres would. It would make the waiting a lot easier.

Pulling out his paperback book, Patrick tried to concentrate on what it said. He'd read the first chapter at least fifteen times, and he still didn't know what the story was about. He didn't really want to read, of course, what he wanted to do was talk. But Pres wanted silence. He looked terrible, Patrick thought, wondering if Pres had slept at all since this thing started. And then, earlier, he'd had to tell Mary Ellen's family what was going on. That couldn't have been easy.

Sighing, Patrick turned back to his book. He knew Pres still didn't want him here, and he couldn't help feeling depressed about it. They'd been through a lot together, and this was the worst. But even though they were in the same room, they were going through this one apart.

Patrick was still struggling through the first page of the book when the telephone rang. He jumped up, knocking over his chair, and followed Pres, who was already halfway to the living room. His mouth went dry as he watched Pres and the two police officers reach for their phones. The sergeant had a new one, one with a speaker, and as Patrick waited to hear the caller's voice, he realized that he had his fingers crossed. He never thought he'd hope to hear from a kidnapper, but that's what he was doing.

"Hello?" Pres's voice was low, but it didn't shake.

"Hey, Pres, this is Sean."

Patrick slowly uncrossed his fingers.

"Sean?"

"Dubrow," Sean said. "How you doing?"

"Uh . . ." Pres frowned. "Listen, Sean, sorry, but I can't talk right now."

"That's okay, I'll only take a second." Sean chuckled. "This is going to sound stupid, but Mary Ellen didn't happen to lose her car, did she?"

"Lose . . . ?" Pres looked baffled. Then, as he realized what Sean was saying, he almost shouted, "You found it? You know where it is?"

"You mean she really lost it?" Sean sounded amused. "How'd she manage that?"

"Never mind how, where is it?" Pres demanded.

"Well, it might be a little hard to find," Sean said, and Patrick could tell he was confused by Pres's tone of voice. "I know. Get on the highway

89

and drive toward St. Cloud. You know that ice cream place, the one that's closed for the winter? I'll meet you there and take you to the car."

In twenty minutes, Pres, Patrick, and Inspector Albright were at the closed ice cream stand, where Sean was waiting in his red Fiero. He was obviously curious about why Patrick was there, and who this strange woman was, but something about the looks on their faces made him keep his questions to himself. In a few more minutes, they pulled up next to the silver-gray car with the orange pinstripes.

"That's it," Pres said, getting out of the inspector's car. "I know the license number."

"Well, great, you've got it back." Sean looked pleased but still confused.

Inspector Albright had been walking around the car; now she stopped and looked at Sean. "Did you touch it?" she asked.

"Well, I . . . I tested the handles," Sean told her, his confusion growing. "You know, to see if it was locked. I think that's all. And I'm sure Kate didn't touch it."

"Kate?"

"My girlfriend," he explained. "She was with me." He looked back and forth between Pres and Patrick, hoping for an explanation. Like, who was this person, for one? And for two, even if the car had been stolen, why was it getting such special treatment? Cars were stolen every day, and that was too bad, but it wasn't the kind of thing people got so tense about. And these three people were definitely tense. "Was there something important in the car when it was stolen?" he asked. "I mean lots of cash or something?"

No one answered his question, but Inspector Albright said, "You didn't happen to find anything near the car, did you? A piece of paper, or a shopping bag, even some cloth torn from a shirt or jacket, maybe?"

"Kate did," Sean told her, suddenly remembering. "She found a hairclip caught on one of these bushes. I didn't look at it very closely, but it sparkled. She still has it if you want to see it."

"Thank you, we might," The inspector glanced around, frowning. Then, almost talking to herself, she said, "They must have brought them here and then switched cars. Not much hope for footprints."

"What about fingerprints?" Pres asked.

"I'll get the lab people on it right away," she said.

Sean's confusion was turning to concern. "Listen," he said, "would somebody mind telling me what's going on? I mean, the car was stolen, but now it's found. And it hasn't been stripped or anything, even the tape deck's still in it. So what's the big deal?" He turned to Patrick. "And I know it's none of my business, but what are you doing here?"

Patrick looked at Pres, who was looking at the inspector. She thought a moment and then smiled at Sean. "Mr. . . . Dubrow, is it?"

Sean nodded.

"My name's Inspector Albright. I'm with the Tarenton Police Department," she told him. "I'm afraid I can't tell you much about what's happening right now. I appreciate you calling Mr. Tilford about the car, though. It may turn out to be a big help."

A big help with what? Sean wondered. But the inspector had said all she was going to say — to him, anyway. He turned again to Pres and Patrick, but the two of them were being about as talkative as clams. Something very strange was going on, he thought, as he headed back to his car. He didn't know what it was, but somehow he did know it wasn't good.

"He knows," Patrick said, as he and Pres and the inspector drove back toward Tarenton.

"How could he?" Pres asked. "Nobody said anything about kidnappng, and it's not the kind of thing Sean — or anybody — would think of."

"I didn't mean that," Patrick said. "I just meant he knows something's happening. And he's going to start asking questions and then the whole squad will be trying to find out what's going on."

"What do you suggest we do — tell them?"

"I don't know." Patrick thought about it. He'd never been a cheerleader, but he knew the squad and he knew that everyone on it thought of it as a second family. They always stuck up for each other, helped each other out, even chewed each other out if they needed it. "Maybe they shouldn't be kept in the dark," he said. "Maybe — since they're like family — they deserve to know."

Pres thought about it, too. He *had* been a cheerleader and he knew exactly what Patrick meant about family. What if something like this had happened when he'd been on the squad? Wouldn't he have wanted to know, just so he could share the waiting and the hoping?

Glancing across at the inspector, Pres said, "I don't think it would hurt to tell them. They wouldn't talk to anyone else about it, and it would be better than having Sean asking all kinds of questions. If he starts doing that, my phone would be ringing so much the kidnappers would never get through." It was a small joke, but Pres smiled when he said it, probably the first time he'd smiled since Saturday night. "Besides," he added, "Patrick's right. They deserve to know."

Inspector Albright nodded. "I'll take care of it tomorrow." Then she added optimistically, "If I still have to."

From the backseat, Patrck looked into the rear-view mirror and met Pres's eyes. They were still smiling, and Patrick breathed a small sigh of relief. Things were as rotten as they could be, but at least the friendship was going to survive.

CHAPTER

9

Mary Ellen heard her stomach growl, tried to ignore it, and finally picked up her sandwich and took a bite. The mind and the body run on completely different wavelengths, she thought. I'm terrified, but I'm still hungry. Too hungry to care that this is a meatloaf sandwich.

Meatloaf. Another nonfast food. Were the kidnappers actually doing their own cooking? Mixing tuna salad, baking meatloaf, scrambling eggs? What about all those hostage situations she'd read about, where the police sent in bags from Burger King and sandwiches from the delicatessen?

But you and Tara aren't those kind of hostages, she reminded herself. There's not a television crew outside waiting to film what happens, there's no hostage expert negotiating with the kidnappers. And if the police do know about this, they don't know where you are. Even you don't know where you are.

In spite of what she'd said to Tara about sitting tight, Mary Ellen was beginning to feel more and more edgy as more time went by. What was happening? Why was it taking so long? The kidnappers hustled her in and out of the other room so fast she never got a chance to hear what they said to Pres, but she'd spoken to him twice now. The first time, maybe they just told him what they'd done. But the second time — wouldn't they have asked him for the money?

Of course, she reminded herself, they must have asked for a lot. Nobody became a kidnapper for pocket money. So Pres was probably selling stocks or something, to get the cash together. And he couldn't have done it yesterday, that was Sunday. It was Monday now, early in the evening. Maybe tomorrow, she thought. Maybe even tonight, something will happen.

The thought took some of the edge off her worries, and Mary Ellen hungrily reached for the second half of her sandwich. That's when she noticed that Tara hadn't touched her food at all. "You're not eating," she commented. "I know it's meatloaf, but try closing your eyes when you take a bite. It helps."

"Nothing helps a meatloaf sandwich but ketchup," Tara remarked. "And they didn't put any on. I looked." She rearranged herself in the chair, trying to find a spot that wasn't lumpy. It was impossible. "Could I have the bed?" she asked. "I feel like lying down."

"Sure." Mary Ellen scooted off and moved to the chair, watching as Tara stretched out on the bed. "There's a ditch running down the middle of the mattress, but at least it's not bumpy."

"Mmm." Tara closed her eyes. "I just feel so tired all of a sudden. And achy."

Mary Ellen stopped eating and studied Tara carefully. She didn't look pale, or flushed, or like she hurt anywhere. The only thing wrong, that she could see, was that Tara's beautiful red hair needed washing. So does yours, she told herself, and anyway, grubby hair doesn't make anyone ache.

Was Tara pretending to feel sick? She'd talked about doing that before, to make the kidnappers get a doctor or take her to one. Maybe she'd decided to go ahead and try it without telling Mary-Ellen.

Reaching for her glass of orange juice, Mary Ellen said, "I'm not surprised that you're tired. We haven't been sleeping much. And if you're aching, you can blame this chair. It's enough to give anyone a permanent pain."

Mary Ellen had convinced herself that it was almost over. And there was no way she would let Tara do anything risky. Not now.

On Tuesday after school, the cheerleaders met in the parking lot before heading to Garrison High School. Coach Engborg was there, counting heads and making sure everyone had a ride. They were all shivering slightly in the cold wind and eager to get going, especially Melissa, who couldn't wait for the chance to cheer. Hope and Olivia were discussing a research paper they both had to do, and Peter was asking Jessica about the college one of her brothers attended.

Only Sean stood alone, leaning against his car and trying to figure out what yesterday meant. Sean wasn't a worrier; as Kate constantly pointed out to him, he tended to let problems roll away like water off a duck's back, instead of meeting them head-on. But in this case, even if he'd wanted to meet it, he had no idea what the problem was. Something was up, though, and it was beginning to bother him. A lot.

Olivia laughed out loud, and Sean looked up. She and Mary Ellen have been friends for a long time, he thought. They probably talk on the phone at least two or three times a week. Olivia would know if anything had happened.

Uncrossing his arms, Sean walked over to where Olivia and Hope were standing. "Hey," he said casually, "I don't suppose Pres and Mary Ellen have set another date for that party yet."

Olivia laughed. "I doubt it. Mary Ellen still has laryngitis and I don't think she'd enjoy whispering through an entire party."

"When did you talk to her?" Sean asked.

"Last night."

"You talked to Mary Ellen last night?"

"Well, no," Olivia said. "I talked to Pres and he told me."

"Why?" Hope asked, noticing the frown on Sean's face. "Is there a problem?"

"I know," Olivia said teasingly. "He's just worried about the party. Come on, Sean, your father's back from his trip, isn't he? Why don't you be the host?"

Sean didn't tease her back, which was unusual,

but before either girl could comment, he'd turned and headed back to his car.

Maybe he was making too much of this, he thought. Mary Ellen had a bad cold. That's why nobody had seen or talked to her. And if an inspector from the police department was spending more time than usual trying to find out who'd stolen Mary Ellen's car, it was probably because the name Tilford had a lot of clout in Tarenton. That had to be all, didn't it?

Sean was still trying to convince himself to let this problem roll off his back, too, when a familiar-looking car rolled into the parking lot. He'd seen the car yesterday, and he'd seen the driver — it was Inspector Albright.

Dressed in corduroy pants, a bulky blue sweater, and a tan down vest, the inspector got out and walked over to Coach Engborg. The two women shook hands, and then walked to the edge of the parking lot, away from the cheerleaders.

Sean watched them intently as they talked, but he wasn't a lip-reader, so all he could do was try to read their expressions. The inspector looked serious but calm. The coach looked calm, too, at first. Then Sean saw her eyes widen, and she ran a hand through her short blonde hair, the way she always did when she was mad or worried. What was it this time? he wondered. Anger or worry?

Coach Engborg glanced at the cheerleaders, then said something to the inspector, who nodded. The two women shook hands again, and Inspector Albright walked back to her car.

Coach Engborg took a deep breath. "All right!" she called out. "Let's get this show on the road. And everyone be sure to drive carefully!"

It was what she always said, but it wasn't the way she always said it. Sean had been hoping she'd sound mad, but she didn't. She sounded worried, and the doubts he'd been pushing down suddenly began to rise again.

By that time, Mary Ellen's doubts were on the rise again, too. She'd been so sure, Monday evening, that today would be the day. But the night went by, and now most of Tuesday was gone, and still nothing had happened.

It was getting harder and harder to convince herself that everything would be all right, but she still might have been able to do it if it hadn't been for Tara.

Tara was sick. For real. Mary Ellen didn't know what it was — it could have been the flu — but it hadn't taken long to see that Tara wasn't faking it. She was too tired to eat, too tired to brush her hair or wash her face, too tired to do anything but lie on the bed. As far as Mary Ellen could tell, she didn't have a fever, but every once in a while she got the shivers, and the two ugly army blankets in the room weren't enough. Then the shivers would pass and Tara would throw off the blankets, not cold anymore, but still tired and achy.

"I feel like somebody stomped on me," she'd said Tuesday morning. "Sometimes I feel like this after coach gives us an extra-hard workout, but it never lasts. A hot shower always gets rid of it."

"It's the flu, I'm sure of it," Mary Ellen told her. "I had it a couple of months ago. You could use tons of hot water and you'd still feel like you've been stomped on."

"How long does it last?"

"About a week," Mary Ellen said. "But don't worry, we'll be out of here before that. Then you can at least feel miserable in your own bed." Tara just nodded, so Mary Ellen tried a joke. "Listen, why don't I tell our 'waiter'? Then you can put that plan of yours into action."

"Plan? Oh, you mean to escape," Tara mumbled. "Forget it. The way I feel now, I couldn't break my way out of a paper bag." She turned on her side, her eyes drifting closed again. "I guess we'll just have to do it your way and wait for whatever happens."

It had been a great game. Garrison was always a tough opponent, and whenever the two teams played, nobody could predict the outcome. This time around, Tarenton had managed to get ahead by three points early in the game, and when the final buzzer sounded, they'd won by those same three points.

Melissa was exhilarated. The Wolves had put another win under their belts, and she'd put another performance under hers. At first, she'd been disappointed that it wasn't a home game, but now that it was over, she was glad. The Tarenton fans were in the minority, of course, but no one would have known it from the way they yelled. The minute the Wolves took the floor, their fans had come alive, making more noise than she'd expected at an away game. Their loyalty made Melissa want to do the absolute best she could, and she'd thrown herself into the routines as if the outcome of the game depended on the cheerleaders. Maybe it did, she thought, just a little bit.

" 'One More Time' went perfectly," Olivia told her as they drove back to Tarenton. "And you were great."

"Thanks," Melissa said. "Everyone was. I think it went even better than at practice." Actually, not quite everyone had been great. Sean had been off. It wasn't that he'd made any drastic mistakes like falling on his face or not being in position when he was supposed to hoist Melissa into the air. But every time she'd been paired with him, she got the feeling that he wasn't really there, that his body was going through the motions while his mind was working overtime in a completely different place. It was very strange, because Sean was about the most "there" person Melissa knew.

As Olivia drove them into town, Melissa thought that maybe that's why Coach Engborg hadn't said anything about the way they'd cheered. The coach was very sharp. She always seemed to know exactly who was "on" and who wasn't, even if the routines went well. Maybe that was why she'd told them all to meet back at the gym instead of going home — so she could give them a pep talk. But *that* didn't make sense. If the coach had picked up on Sean's lack of concentration, she wouldn't talk to the whole squad about it.

"What's this meeting about, do you know?" Melissa asked as they pulled into the high school parking lot.

Olivia shook her head. "She's got something on her mind, that's obvious. I mean, we were close to perfect this afternoon, except for Sean. He was a little bit out of it, but you needed a microscope to see it."

Melissa smiled. The captain of the squad was very sharp, too.

"And she didn't say a word," Olivia went on, pulling into a parking space. "Of course, she's not the kind to jump up and down, but when we do a good job, she usually tells us. Anyway," she added, "I just hope this is a short meeting. I've got tons of homework."

The two girls got out of the car and walked into the gym. Jessica, Hope, and Peter were already there. Nobody knew what the meeting was about, but everybody wanted to get it over with and get home. Sean came in a couple of minutes later and leaned against a wall, not joining in the talk about how hungry everyone was and how much homework they all had to do.

Something's bothering him, Melissa thought. Maybe he and Kate had a fight. Of course, they argued at least once a day, and it never seemed to make a difference in their relationship, but maybe this was a serious argument. She was wondering whether she ought to go talk to him, to see if she could help, when Coach Engborg came into the gym.

"Not here," the coach said. "Come with me, please. To my office."

Mystified, the cheerleaders left the gym and followed her down the hall. The coach's office was more like an oversized closet, and with six teenagers and three adults in it, it became an overstuffed closet.

Three adults, Sean thought. Mrs. Oetjen (Tarenton High's principal), the coach, and standing behind the coach's desk, Inspector Albright.

Sean looked at the inspector and she gave him a smile, the kind of smile you give someone you've met but don't really know. A polite smile.

Sean didn't smile back. He wasn't trying to be rude, he just couldn't do it. Because it was obvious — even before the coach cleared her throat and said, "I'm afraid there's some bad news" — that something had gone terribly wrong.

CHAPTER

10

Ardith Engborg cleared her throat again and motioned to the woman behind the desk. "This is Inspector Albright from the Tarenton Police Department," she said. "I'm going to let her tell you what has happened, since she knows much more about it than I do."

All eyes shifted to the inspector, the last movement anyone made from the moment she began speaking. She had a lovely voice — low and musical — but the words that voice was saying sounded as if they'd been written by a monster.

Standing like statues, their homework and hunger forgotten, the cheerleaders heard this nice-looking woman tell them that Mary Ellen and Tara had been kidnapped and were being held for ransom.

"Mr. Tilford — Pres — has been contacted twice," she said, after describing what had happened so far. "We're almost certain that the next time they call, they'll tell him how much money they want. After that, things should move more quickly. Until then, I have to ask you not to speak to anyone at all about this. Naturally, the kidnappers warned Pres not to go to the police," she went on with a wry smile. "He and his friend Patrick were smart enough not to listen to them, but we can't take any chances on the kidnappers finding out, so that's the main reason for asking you to keep quiet." She stopped and waited a moment, but no one said anything. "Any questions?" she asked.

Still no one spoke. They didn't trust their voices yet.

Finally, Coach Engborg ran her fingers through her hair and said, "You keep saying kidnappers, in the plural. How many do you think there are?"

"The one who calls always says 'we.'" Inspector Albright told her. "Of course, that could mean two or twelve, we've no way of knowing right now. But my guess is no more than three. The more people involved, the more chances of something going wrong." Another small smile. "As far as I'm concerned, though, they've already made a big mistake by keeping the girls in Tarenton."

"They're here?" Olivia asked, shocked out of her silence. "They're somewhere in town?"

The inspector nodded. "Pres tried to keep the caller on the phone long enough to trace the exact location, but it didn't work the first time. There'll be at least one more call, though, and probably two, so he'll get another shot at it."

"If they're in town, then maybe somebody's seen something," Peter said.

"That's right," Hope agreed. "Tarenton isn't that big, and it doesn't seem like the kind of place you could hide a kidnapping for very long."

"That's why I call it a mistake," Inspector Albright said. "Why they did it this way, I don't know. I'm just glad they did. We've been covering sections of the town ever since we found out the call was local. I don't want you to start asking questions," she repeated, "but naturally, if you hear anything, if anyone says something to you that might be a lead, don't hesitate to get in touch with the department immediately."

There wasn't much more to say. The cheerleaders had been told, and now they couldn't do anything but wait for whatever happened next. But they went on standing there in the small office, not quite ready to step outside and join the real world again.

The inspector slipped on her vest and shook hands with the coach. Before she left, she turned to the cheerleaders and said, "I think you should know that it wasn't my idea to tell you about this. Pres and Patrick wanted you to be told. They said you're family, and you deserve to know." Smiling, she added, "It may not feel like it right now, but that's a big compliment."

"Are you listening, Mr. Tilford?"

Pres didn't bother to answer. "Let me speak to Mary Ellen. And Tara," he said firmly. "Or I might as well hang up right now."

It was Wednesday morning, about the time that

most people were showering themselves awake and thinking about breakfast and the day to come. In Pres and Mary Ellen's house, time was turned upside down. Pres had eaten a bowl of cereal at three in the morning while the inspector dozed on the couch. When she woke up, he'd taken a short nap, then a quick shower. The sergeant had arrived at five, and when the phone rang, they'd all been eating crackers and sliced cheese. Nights and days were running together, and Pres knew it was early morning only because of the light and the birds.

As for thinking about the day to come, Pres had no plans beyond sitting, and hoping, and waiting for the telephone to ring. He leaped to grab the receiver. "Hello," he said, took a deep breath, and went on.

"If you want me to listen to you," he said now, "I have to speak to Tara, too."

There was a short silence, and then he heard Tara's voice. "Hi, Pres, it's me, Tara. I'm not exactly Miss Sunshine anymore, but I'm okay. Nobody's hurt me."

Almost immediately, Mary Ellen came on. "I'm all right, too, Pres."

This time, Pres had no chance to say anything, There was another quick pause, then the kidnapper was back. "Let's get down to business, Mr. Tilford."

"You forgot to ask me if I'm listening," Pres reminded him.

The kidnapper ignored the comment. "Five hundred thousand," he said. "We could have asked for more. We know you've got it."

Inspector Albright was making a slow, pulling motion with her hand. She wanted Pres to keep the conversation going as long as he could. Pres nodded. "I don't have it lying around the house," he said slowly. "But I can get it. It'll take time, of course."

"Of course," the kidnapper agreed. "And we've got patience. But it'll run out in twenty-four hours." A click, and he was gone.

"The guy sure knows how to mince words," Sergeant Wells remarked. "Too bad — there was no time for a trace."

"Sorry," Pres said. "I couldn't think of anything to talk about."

"It's all right. You tried," Inspector Albright told him. At least Pres hadn't argued with her this time. It made the waiting and the worrying easier to bear. "Anyway, you'll get another chance at it. In twenty-four hours."

"Right." Pres touched his toes a couple of times, then shook his head as if to clear it. "And I've finally got something to do," he said, and reached for the telephone to start making arrangements for the money.

There had been a time when girls' basketball at Tarenton didn't attract enough people to fill a garage, but that time was long gone. The team had always taken itself seriously, and now that it was well on its way to the county championship, everyone else was taking it seriously, too.

Thursday was a make or break game, and Wednesday afternoon's cheerleading practice was especially important. There was a new routine to work on, one that included the entire pom-pon squad. It was intricate and complicated and it needed everyone's complete concentration.

It didn't get it. Two steps into the routine, Coach Engborg clapped her hands loudly. "Off!" she called out. "Your timing's way off. Start again, please, and think!"

Think? Olivia had been thinking since yesterday afternoon and she would have given anything to stop. Her mind, she discovered, had a will of its own. Every time she tried to switch the subject, it went right back to Mary Ellen and Tara. They must be so scared. Would they be all right? Where were they? What were *they* thinking about?

Another hand clap from the coach. "Olivia! It's two beats before the cartwheel, not five. You almost kicked Diana's teeth out."

"Sorry." Olivia looked at Diana Tucker, who was smoothing her blonde hair and looking awfully pleased for somone who'd almost been kicked in the mouth. I guess hearing me get chewed out makes her happy, Olivia thought.

"Again, please," Coach Engborg called.

Olivia didn't goof up this time, but it was just luck. As she flipped and cartwheeled and stamped her feet, she kept thinking of Mary Ellen and Tara. She'd cheered with both of them and she knew that Pres and Patrick were right — they were family. How could you concentrate on anything when part of your family was in danger?

As the practice went on, all of the cheerleaders were singled out for criticism from the coach. Sean leaped when he shouldn't have, not once, but five times. Jessica consistently led her line of pompon girls in the wrong direction, as if she suddenly couldn't tell her left from her right. Hope was always one beat behind everyone else, and Peter almost dropped Melissa, who moved like a piece of cardboard.

Coach Engborg understood why they were so off, of course. She was off, too, which was why she was harder on them than usual. All of them were having trouble for the same reason — they were worried and frightened.

They practiced for an hour and a half, but the routine never got off the ground, and the coach finally decided to leave it there for the time being. "All right," she said, after the last disastrous run-through. "That's enough for today. The game's tomorrow. I've heard of people learning foreign languages in their sleep, so let's see if you can make scientific history by being the first to learn a routine the same way."

As they were leaving the gym, Diana, who hadn't made a single mistake, turned to Melissa. "Coach Engborg isn't usually sarcastic, is she? But I guess I can't blame her. It must be hard to have your entire varsity squad turn into klutzes right before your very eyes."

Melissa just nodded. What could she say to defend herself? She couldn't tell what had happened to Mary Ellen and Tara, and even if she could, she didn't think it would help. Like the other cheerleaders, Melissa was scared and upset. But there was something else that had changed her from the graceful, confident girl of the day before into what Diana so sweetly described as a klutz. The something else was guilt.

First, she'd been glad that Tara had the flu, because it gave her a chance to shine, a chance to be out there with the other cheerleaders where she thought she belonged. But worse than that, she'd been hoping — she had to admit it — that Tara wouldn't get well for a few more days, so she could keep on shining.

Now she'd learned that Tara wasn't sick, that she and Mary Ellen had been kidnapped and could possibly be killed. Melissa knew it wasn't her fault, but she also felt that she'd never shine again. Tara was the one who belonged; she was a part of that family, while Melissa was just a visitor.

Unlike Melissa, Sean wasn't feeling the slightest bit of guilt. And although he was as concerned as everyone else, it wasn't concern that had made him flub almost every step in the routine. It was memory. Or rather, the lack of it.

Tara and Mary Ellen were kidnapped late Saturday afternoon, according to Inspector Albright. They'd been forced to drive into the hills, and then they were put in another car and taken back into Tarenton. And where had Sean been at that time? He'd been with Kate. He'd dropped her off at her house and then tried to hurry to get to the pregame warm-up. Except he couldn't hurry because he'd gotten stuck behind that van. That dark-colored van with the license plate. The license plate that said . . . what?

He thought he'd never forget it, but just before today's practice, when it suddenly hit him that that might have been the actual kidnap van, he discovered that the numbers and letters had vanished from his memory.

Frowning in concentration, he went into the locker room. By the time he'd finished showering and getting dressed, he still couldn't remember. Of course, he could tell the inspector about it anyway, but the information wouldn't be much help without the license number. He'd seen the driver at that traffic light, but the only thing that stuck in his mind about him were his hands, tight on the steering wheel. And there had to be hundreds of dark-colored vans around. The license was the key.

Suddenly, Sean lifted his head. Peter, who'd been waiting for a lift home, was standing in front of him, hair combed, jacket on, ready to go.

"Sorry," Sean said. "I was thinking."

"Yeah. I guess we're both thinking about the same thing," Peter said.

"Mm. What do you do when you forget something, like a phone number?" Sean asked. "And there's no way to look it up?"

Peter frowned. "I thought we were talking about Mary Ellen and Tara."

"We are," Sean said, and told him about the van.

"That's great!" Peter said excitedly, "Let's see, what's the best way to remember something? My mother always says don't try and it'll come to you, but that never works for me. And numbers — I don't know, they're tricky. With names, I sort of run the alphabet slowly through my head, and . . ."

"Slowly! That's it!" Sean jumped up from the

locker room bench. "The license plate was 'something-something-something SLO!' How could I forget? I was in a hurry and the van was creeping along in front of me so slowly I could have taken a nap!" He searched his pockets and came up empty-handed. "Got some change?" he asked. "I'll use the pay phone down the hall to call Pres's house and tell them."

Five minutes later, Pres, Inspector Albright, and Sergeant Wells put down their phones and shared the first smile of hope since the whole ordeal had started.

"This is wonderful," the inspector said, her calm eyes sparkling with the anticipation of solving the case. "First Mr. Dubrow finds Mary Ellen's car, and now he may have spotted the van."

"Sign him up," the sergeant suggested with a chuckle. "The guy's got possibilities."

Pres shook his head. "I think Sean would rather have a medal," he said. "It attracts more attention." While the sergeant called the station with the news, Pres followed the inspector into the kitchen. "Do you think there's a chance they'll find it?"

"There's always a chance," Inspector Albright said, pouring herself a cup of coffee. "The motor vehicle bureau's running a check right now. And if they don't come up with a registration, the squad cars will be on the lookout."

"What will you do if you find it?"

She sipped her coffee, then added more cream. "That depends on where we find it, who it belongs to, a lot of different things," she said. "We couldn't just barge into someone's house or apartment to search. Not without more evidence. There's no law against driving a van up into the hills and down into Tarenton. We'd have to sit tight and watch."

"That doesn't sound so bad for once," Pres admitted. "I mean, I would have been worried if you said you *were* going to break down somebody's door. That could be dangerous."

Inspector Albright looked at him over the rim of her coffee cup, her eyes smiling. "I'm glad to hear you say that," she told him. "Two days ago, I might have had to handcuff you to keep you from looking for that van yourself."

Pres felt slightly embarrassed, remembering how belligerent he'd been. He still wasn't completely convinced that putting the kidnappers off — asking for time, demanding to speak to Tara — was the right way to go, but the inspector had convinced him of one thing: she cared.

"Just remember, though," Inspector Albright said now. "If we have to break down somebody's door, we will. Because Mary Ellen and Tara are already in danger."

CHAPTER

When Mary Ellen and Tara were taken back to their room after talking to Pres, Tara went straight to bed and lay down, falling into a kind of semidoze. Mary Ellen sat on the footstool, her back against the edge of the chair, and looked at her friend. Tara wasn't any worse, but she wasn't any better, either.

Thnking back to her own bout with the flu, Mary Ellen tried to remember if she'd felt as bad as Tara did. Had she been as pale? Well, she hadn't spent much time looking in the mirror, but Pres told her that her face matched the whites of her eyes. Had she felt stomped on, like Tara did? Yes, definitely, she'd felt trampled. She hadn't been able to eat, and when she slept, which was most of the time, she woke up more tired than ever.

Yes, it's the flu and it's terrible, but that's all it is, Mary Ellen told herself. Don't start imagining that it's anything worse or you'll go crazy. You got over it, and so will Tara.

Of course, it was a lot easier getting over it in her own bed, with cool clean sheets, not in some sagging bed with no sheets at all. And Pres had been there, bringing her tea and ginger ale and magazines.

When the door opened and the short kidnapper appeared with their food, Mary Ellen stood up and faced him for the first time. She hadn't realized it until he walked in, but she was mad. "My friend is sick," she said, not taking her eyes off his masked face. "I think it's the flu. She needs lots of things to drink. And she aches. You must have some aspirin or something around here, along with the meatloaf and the potato chips."

The kidnapper set down the tray of food and glanced briefly at Tara.

"She can't eat that," Mary Ellen said, pointing to the baked beans and hotdogs. She needs light food — broth, Jell-O, crackers."

The kidnapper was already at the door.

"What she really needs is a doctor," Mary Ellen said to his back. "I think it's the flu, but I don't know for certain. And if she gets any sicker, the next time you call, I won't tell my husband that we're fine."

Mary Ellen knew that if they held a gun to her head, she'd probably tell Pres she couldn't be happier, but she was suddenly so furious that she made the threat without even thinking. And once she made it, she felt better, not that there was any reaction from the kidnapper. He just opened the door and went out as if he hadn't heard a word she'd said.

"That was like talking to a wall," she complained, pacing around the room.

"Mm." Tara wadded up one of the blankets and stuck it under her head. "I enjoyed it, though. In fact, you sounded like me when you were talking about the doctor. Are you sure you haven't decided to put my escape plan into action?"

Mary Ellen flopped back down onto the footstool and shook her head. "I just got mad," she said. "If they want the money, they ought to take good care of us. No, I haven't changed my mind about escaping."

"I haven't either." Tara smiled and lowered her voice. "Didn't you hear me give that clue to Pres?"

"What clue?"

"I said I wasn't Miss Sunshine anymore," Tara reminded her. "That was to let him know we're in a dark place." Seeing the look on Mary Ellen's face, she smiled again. "I know, it wasn't very good. He probably just thought I meant that I was depressed, but it was the best I could do on such short notice."

Mary Ellen shook her head. "I should have known you wouldn't give up."

"Well, don't worry about it, it was a lousy clue." Tara unfolded the other blanket and wrapped it around her shoulders. "And like I said, I feel so bad that I couldn't escape unless they unlocked the door. Even then, I might have to go on my hand and knees."

Tara drifted off to sleep again, and Mary Ellen

leaned her head back against the chair, closing her own eyes. This was one of the worst parts about being here. The minutes went by like hours, and there was nothing to do but wait and think and wonder. How was Pres? How were her family and friends? And would she ever see them again?

By Thursday afternoon, the hope brought by Sean's news about the van had started to fade. One dark-colored van with the letters SLO had turned up on the motor vehicle bureau's list, but it was without an engine and had been for a year. Three more — all from out of town — had the right letters, but were the wrong color. The patrol cars had been notified to be on the lookout for the van, but so far they hadn't spotted one.

"But it's here in Tarenton," Pres said. "It has to be. Unless the kidnappers have moved somewhere else."

Inspector Albright shook her head. "As of the last call, they were still in town. They could decide to change locations, I suppose, but it wouldn't be a very bright thing to do — too much chance of the girls being seen."

They were sitting at the kitchen table, drinking milk this time instead of coffee. Patrick was with them, having once again left his company in the hands of other people. Now he said, "Maybe they changed the license plates."

"If they did that, then they're not as stupid as I hoped," Pres commented. "I mean, as far as they know, nobody suspects that van, so why should they bother?"

"Just being cautious," Inspector Albright said. "And they're not stupid, unfortunately." She thought a minute. "There's another possibility. They could have painted the van before they used it for the kidnapping." She picked up the computer printout listing the vans with the right letters and scanned it quickly. "One's tan and two are white. I'll notify the other towns' police departments to check them out. At least they're all in this state, so it won't take forever. But it will take time," she added on her way out of the kitchen, "so sit tight."

Pres reached for his milk. "You'd think by now I'd be good at sitting tight, but I'm getting worse, not better." He started to drink, then set the glass down and got up restlessly. "The guy said twenty-four hours. It's way past that, so why doesn't he call? I've got the money, all he has to do is call and tell me what to do with it."

"According to the inspector, he's doing what he did in the beginning," Patrick said. "Letting you sweat." He stood up, too, feeling restless himself. It was great that Pres had finally spoken to Tara, but his relief at knowing she was all right had started to wear off. Reaching for his keys, he said, "I think I'll go out for a while, maybe pick up some soda or something."

Pres nodded, and Patrick went out, feeling slightly guilty at leaving his friend to sweat it out alone. But he'd been keeping everything inside so long, being calm and reasonable, that he suddenly had to move.

The sodas had just been an excuse, and Patrick

drove past three stores before he remembered that he was going to get some. By that time he was near the high school, on the side where the gym was. Not sure why, he pulled into the parking lot and sat there, staring at the open doors.

In a few minutes, Jessica appeared, standing in the doorway as if she wanted a breath of fresh air. She was wearing her uniform, and her long brown hair was pulled back and tied with a piece of fuzzy red yarn. She didn't look anything like Tara, but when Patrick closed his eyes, he imagined that she was Tara.

When he opened his eyes, Jessica was walking toward his truck. She didn't know what she was going to say to him, she just knew she had to say something. After all, he'd been her boyfriend once, and they were still friends. He must be hurting a lot right now.

"Hi," she said when she reached the truck. "I was going to ask if there's any news, but I can tell by your face that the answer is no."

"There's a little," Patrick said, and without going into detail he brought her up to date on what was happening. "The guy was supposed to call this morning to see if Pres had the money, but he didn't. We're back to the waiting game."

"When he does call, then things should start to move pretty fast, shouldn't they?"

"I hope so. I *guess* I hope so," Patrick corrected himself. "Things will start to move, but that's kind of scary. I guess I'm afraid the kidnappers will panic or something once it's almost over."

Jessica shivered, not only from the cool wind. After all, this wasn't a normal, everyday exchange of money between civilized human beings.

"I'd better get back," Patrick said. "I want to be there when the call comes."

Jessica glanced at her watch. "I have to go, too. The game starts in ten minutes." She looked toward the school, then back at Patrick. "This is a stupid question, but how are you?"

"I've been better," Patrick told her. "And it's not a stupid question. There aren't that many people who know what's happening, and it helps to talk to someone who does."

Jessica smiled. Then she leaned into the open window of the truck and kissed his cheek. "Tell Pres we're thinking of him," she said, squeezing his arm. "We're thinking of all of you."

When Jessica walked back to the school, she found Diana standing in the open doorway, swishing her pompons back and forth against her skirt. "That was sweet," Diana commented. "Sweet, but underhanded, don't you think? After all, Tara's only been out sick for a few days. Are you sure Patrick's forgotten her already?"

Jessica stared at her. If you only knew, she thought. Then she decided that even if Diana *did* know what had happened, she'd probably still think Jessica was taking advantage of it. "You know, Diana," she said, "I just realized why you didn't make the squad, and why Melissa's the alternate instead of you."

"Oh?"

"Mm. It's not because you're not talented, even

I'll admit you are," Jessica told her. "It's because you're missing the one thing that every varsity cheerleader has to have. It's about the size of a fist, it's in the chest, and it goes thump-thump. But you don't have one, so you probably don't even know what I'm talking about. Shall I spell it for you?"

Diana stopped swishing the pompons, turned on her heel, and started walking away. "You don't have to spell it," she called back over her shoulder. "But if you and the rest of the squad have any heart at all, you'd better put more of it into the routine than you did at practice yesterday."

Unfortunately, Diana was right. The cheerleaders' hearts hadn't been in their work at practice, and they were still missing when the game started that afternoon. Even the easy cheers, the ones they did at every game, didn't go right. They were either too fast or too slow, they jumped on the wrong beat and forgot so many words the fans were the only ones chanting half the time. It was as if each cheerleader had invented new steps and a new system of counting and hadn't bothered to tell anyone else.

During a quick break, Olivia saw Duffy sitting partway up the stands. He'd done exactly what she asked and stayed away from her, but of course he didn't stay away from the games. Covering them was part of his job.

Duffy saw her watching him, raised his eyebrows, and gave her a questioning look, as if asking what had gone wrong with the varsity squad.

Olivia shrugged, pretending to be as mystified

as he was. It would have been nice, she thought, to tell him what was happening. Or Walt. Each of them, in his own way, would have been able to cheer her up. But she was the one who'd told them to leave her alone, so she'd just have to live with it and figure out some way to cheer herself up.

Just before she went back on the floor to start the new routine, Olivia gave Duffy a thumbs-up signal. We'll be better this time, she was saying.

But they weren't better. The routine wasn't quite the disaster it had been at practice, but it came close. The team and the fans were so pumped up they didn't need any encouragement at all, which was lucky, since they didn't get any.

"We might as well have not bothered to come," Diana fumed when the game was over and everyone was leaving. Once again, she'd done her part perfectly. "I was embarrassed to be out there!"

"There's a solution to that," Sean told her. "Next time, don't come."

"Me?" Diana's eyes widened. "Why should I quit? I'm not the one causing the problems." Giving Melissa a scathing look, she said, "Coach Engborg not only needs a new alternate, she needs a whole new squad."

Before Diana had disappeared down the hall, Melissa was in tears. Hope and Jessica patted her on the shoulder and told her not to pay any attention. Peter and Sean shook their heads and stalked off toward the locker room.

We're falling apart, Olivia thought, frowning at the whole scene. I'm the captain. I'd better think of some way to get us back together again.

* * *

When Patrick got back to Pres's house, he found Pres in the kitchen, exactly where he'd left him. The milk carton was almost empty, but otherwise, nothing had changed.

"No call, huh?" he said, sitting at the table.

"Not even a wrong number," Pres said. He ran his hands through his hair and looked around. "Where's the soda? I'll turn into a cow if I drink any more milk."

"What soda?"

"The soda you went out to get, remember?"

Patrick looked so blank-faced that Pres almost laughed. "Never mind," he said. "I think there are a few more cans stuck away somewhere in here. When I thought we were having the party, I bought enough for an army. I can't believe we drank it all."

"I'll go get some now," Patrick offered.

"Forget it." Pres opened a cabinet door and poked among the boxes of cereal and rice. "This gives me something to do." He was on his hands and knees, checking behind soup cans when the inspector came in.

"News," she said, holding out a piece of note-paper.

Pres stood up, a can of soup in one hand. "Good news?"

"Better than nothing. I just heard from those three towns. Two of the vans check out fine. The third one has a license plate of '987-SLO' and it's listed as being tan. But," she added, "according to a neighbor, when the owner left home ten days ago, the van was navy blue."

"So now they're driving a navy blue van, and they've changed the plates?" Patrick asked.

"It's a strong possibility," the inspector agreed. "And now we can look for a van that was painted recently. Unless it was a super-professional job, which I doubt, we're bound to find some tan paint somewhere on it. Don't worry," she said to Pres, "we won't go scraping paint off people's vans in broad daylight."

Pres barely heard her. "The owner," he said. "Who's the owner?"

Inspector Albright looked at her notes. "It's registered to a Martin Wyman. We're running a check on his driver's license right now."

Martin Wyman, Pres thought. He wondered if Martin Wyman's was the soft, smooth voice that had jolted him into another world on Saturday night.

"Nothing may turn up on his driver's license," the inspector was saying, "but at least it'll tell us what he looks — " She stopped talking and headed back for the living room, Pres and Patrick right behind her. The phone was ringing.

CHAPTER

12

The voice that Pres heard when he picked up the phone belonged to the kidnapper, that much he knew. But it had an angry edge to it, and the usual words — "Are you listening, Mr. Tilford?" — were missing.

"I thought I told you. I thought I warned you," the kidnapper said.

"I don't know what you're talking about," Pres answered, which was the truth.

"You weren't listening, were you, Mr. Tilford. That was a big mistake."

Pres shifted impatiently. "Would you get to the point?"

"Sure, here's the point. The point is, we know you've been to the police!"

Caught off guard, Pres nearly dropped the phone. He glanced over at the inspector, who shook her head at him. He didn't need to be told to lie, but could he pull it off?

"And here's another point," the kidnapper went on. "By going to the police, you just might have ruined our deal, did you ever think of that?"

"Wait a minute!" Pres was angry now and he didn't try to hide it. He'd been mad since the beginning, mad and scared. But for the moment, he forgot about his fear and let loose with the anger. "I don't know who's been giving you your information, but they got it wrong. So why don't you just stop playing games and tell me what to do with this money? Because I've got it. And if you want it, you'll have to do something about it. So it's up to you. If anybody ruins this deal, it'll be you, not me!"

Breathing hard, Pres waited for an answer. But after a second of silence, the kidnapper hung up.

"Try not to worry," Inspector Albright said, seeing the look on Pres's face. "He was just testing you."

"Testing me?" Pres's anger had vanished, and the fear was back, stronger than ever. "How can you be so sure? I *have* been to the police, there are two of you in my house right now and dozens of others looking for the van. How can you be so positive he doesn't know about it?"

Sergeant Wells leaned back in his chair and reached for his coffee cup. "He didn't say, 'we saw you go to the police station Saturday night,' " he pointed out mildly. "He didn't say 'we saw a man and a woman arrive at your house the next day and they haven't left yet.' All he said was, 'you've been to the police.' "

"He wasn't specific," the inspector agreed. "He's just guessing."

127

"But why now?" Pres asked, unconvinced. "Why would he wait this long?"

"Maybe he just wants to make sure you're scared enough to follow his orders when he finally tells you what to do with the money," Patrick said. "Or maybe he's just making sure you don't suddenly *do* decide to go to the police."

"I shouldn't have gotten so mad," Pres said. "I made *him* mad and that's why he hung up. Now we don't know what's going to happen. I might have ruined it all."

"Your reaction was perfect," the inspector told him. "You were very convincing." She stood up and walked over to Pres. "They did this for the money, money that you have. Don't forget that. They're not going to quit just because you yelled at them."

Pres took a deep breath, trying to calm down. He wanted to believe her, but he couldn't, not quite. She said he'd been convincing. Well, so had the kidnapper. And if they really did know he'd been to the police, what did that mean for Mary Ellen and Tara?

The girls' basketball team won their important game in spite of poor support from the cheerleaders. Afterwards, the locker room was full of laughter and congratulations as the team relived their best shots of the afternoon.

Only Hope, Olivia, Jessica, and Melissa were quiet, staying out of the celebration and trying to stay out of sight in the hope that no one would comment on their performance. When the locker room finally emptied out, the four of them sat down on the hard wooden benches and stared glumly at each other.

"We were terrible," Jessica said finally. "What are we going to do?"

"I don't see how we can do anything until we know what's going to happen with Tara and Mary Ellen," Hope said. "I can't think, I can't study, and when I try to play the violin, it sounds like I've never played one before in my life."

Melissa's eyes kept filling up with tears. She managed to blink them back before they fell, but she didn't say anything. If she started talking, she knew there'd be no holding the tears back.

Olivia sighed. The squad had gone through a lot of things together, but this was the worst. Coach Engborg understood, Olivia knew that, but Olivia also knew the coach must be disappointed in them. She hadn't said a word after the game, and if things had been normal, she'd have said plenty. And what if things never got back to normal? What would they do then — just keep getting worse and worse until there was no point in going on?

"So what are we going to do?" Jessica asked again.

Olivia stood up. "We're going to have a meeting," she announced. "The six of us. At Benny's." She looked at her watch. "In fifteen minutes. I'll go tell the guys. Be there!" she called back as she hurried to the door.

Fifteen minutes later, the six cheerleaders were huddled around a back table at Benny's. They'd sat at this same table hundreds of times in the past, ordering burgers and fries from the same waiter. Yet they were all thinking how strange it seemed now, because Tara wasn't with them. No one said anything, though. Since they'd learned of the kidnapping, they'd each crept into a private place in their minds, not able to communicate even with each other. It showed in their routines, and it showed now, as they sat in silence.

"All right," Olivia said, straightening up and sounding very much like Coach Engborg. "We've got to do something." She didn't need to explain what she was talking about; everyone understood.

"Any suggestions?" she asked.

The others shook their heads and Melissa sniffed.

"I hope you're not still upset by what Diana said," Jessica told her. "She's always going to be jealous because you made alternate and she didn't."

"Right," Sean agreed. "And remember, all her remarks bypass her excuse for a brain and start right at her mouth."

"I know." Melissa managed a shaky smile. "But that's not it." She took a deep breath and then told them how guilty she'd been feeling.

"I think that's normal," Hope said gently.

"Of course it is," Olivia said. "When Tara didn't show up at practice that day, I was mad because I thought she'd started getting irresponsible again. Then when I found out what really happened, I felt like a real creep."

"You thought Tara had the flu. Everybody did," Peter pointed out. "And nobody blames you for being glad for a chance to cheer."

"But it isn't just that," Melissa explained. "It's

every time I start to cheer, I feel like it should be Tara and not me. She's the one who really belongs out there with you guys. I feel like I don't have any right to be taking her place."

"Now that's *not* normal," Jessica said bluntly. "If you didn't belong, Coach Engborg wouldn't have chosen you. And if you didn't belong, you wouldn't be sitting here with us now. Just ask — " she stopped, swallowed, and then smiled wryly. "I was going to say 'just ask Tara.' Well, you can't, but I know what she'd say, anyway."

Peter nodded. "She'd tell you she's glad you're the alternate because you're the only one she'd trust to take her place. Because you *do* belong." He smiled to himself. "Of course, if she'd seen the way we've been performing, she might change her mind. About all of us."

"That's it," Olivia said. "Tara doesn't lose her temper, but I have a feeling that if she knew the way we'd fallen apart, she'd really chew us out. And so would Mary Ellen." She doused her hamburger with ketchup and took a big bite. "Can you imagine if they'd walked into the gym this afternoon and seen us tripping all over ourselves?" she went on. "They'd think they were in the wrong school. They'd be ashamed. They'd be embarrassed, they'd — "

"We get the point," Sean interrupted her. "What's the solution?"

"The solution is to believe that everything's going to be all right, and that any day now, they *are* going to walk into the gym," Olivia said. "And we've got to be ready for them."

Sean thought about this. In his jacket pocket

was the butterfly hair clip that Kate had found near Mary Ellen's car. Neither Pres nor Patrick had recognized it. But Kate, whom Sean had told about the kidnapping because he trusted her completely, was sure it belonged to one of the girls. "You keep it," she'd said. "When this is all over and they're safe, you can give it back." She hadn't said "if" they're safe, she'd said "when."

"Let's call an extra practice," he said now.

The others stared at him. They knew he was dedicated to the squad, but nobody thought they'd ever hear him actually suggest an extra practice. He laughed at the looks on their faces and reached for a french fry. "Olivia's right," he told them. "We've got to be in good shape when Mary Ellen and Tara get back. And I hate to admit it, but regular practice just isn't going to do the trick."

"Tomorrow morning, an hour before school starts," Olivia said. "I'll call Coach Engborg and get permission to have the gym. Now everybody eat," she ordered. "Good routines don't get done on empty stomachs."

"Is that quote from Coach Engborg?" Peter asked.

"No," Olivia admitted. "I just made it up."

Everyone laughed, a cautious, hopeful laugh. Then they reached for their food.

"I don't believe it." Mary Ellen looked in disgust at the tray that had just been brought in. "Salami sandwiches. Haven't those two ever heard of soup?"

Tara raised her head and peered at the food. "I like salami," she said wistfully. "But my stom-

132

ach's forgotten about that. I think my stomach's forgotten about food completely."

"No aspirin, either," Mary Ellen remarked. "I told him you're sick. He doesn't have to be a doctor to see that you're sick. What kind of people are they, anyway?"

"Kidnappers," Tara said, and the two girls shared a smile.

"That was a stupid question," Mary Ellen admitted. "I guess I shouldn't complain."

"Not complain?" Tara raised her head again. "You've been kidnapped. Can you think of a better reason to complain?"

"I just meant that hearing me gripe doesn't help you any."

"I don't mind," Tara said, lying back down. "It's better than having you so quiet, like you were in the beginning."

"I was scared," Mary Ellen told her. "I'm just as scared as ever, but . . . I don't know. We've been waiting so long, Tara. I'm tired of being quiet and I'm tired of waiting."

"I know," Tara said. "I've decided there's one good thing about being sick like this — I sleep a lot. I thought I'd have nightmares, but I don't even remember dreaming. So sleeping keeps me from thinking about my parents and Patrick." She looked at her friend. "You don't sleep much, do you? You must be thinking of your family and Pres all the time."

Mary Ellen nodded. "I'm tired of doing that, too," she said softly. "I want to see them again."

"Well, it won't be long."

"How do you know that?" Mary Ellen asked.

"I don't really," Tara admitted. "But it better not be long. Because if we're still here when I get well, then we're going to escape whether you like it or not."

It's like being under siege, Patrick thought, looking around Pres's living room. Empty coffee cups, crumpled paper napkins, all of us nervous and looking at the clock every thirty seconds. Even Inspector Albright was tense. She hid it pretty well, but he'd caught her sneaking a peek at her watch a few too many times. And there was Pres, standing by while the sergeant took photographs of the ransom money — more money than Patrick had ever seen in his life. Pres's shirt was wrinkled and he need a shave — something else Patrick thought he'd never see.

It was the waiting, he knew that. They'd heard nothing since the last phone call, when the kidnapper had accused Pres of going to the police. Patrick was almost sure it had been a bluff, but ever since the call, he'd noticed that the waiting was getting harder on everyone. Because they could never be a hundred percent sure, not until they got another call.

It didn't help, either, that the police still hadn't found a van with some telltale tan paint underneath its navy blue. Of course, as the inspector said, they could hardly go scraping paint off vans in the middle of the day, but Patrick couldn't help wondering what was taking so long. How many navy blue vans were there in Tarenton, anyway? Unless it turned out to be the wrong van. Then they'd be back to square one.

That's the wrong way to think, Patrick told himself. It's the right van, it has to be. And the kidnappers will call back, any minute now. They want their money. So stop chewing your fingernails and make yourself useful.

Patrick was busying himself picking up Styrofoam cups and paper plates and dumping them in a trash bag when Pres walked over to him. "You don't have to do that," Pres said.

"Yes I do." Patrick wadded up some napkins and tossed them in the bag. "I can't leave until something happens. You're stuck with me, and I figure I might as well earn my keep."

"Okay," Pres said. "When you're finished with that, why don't you vacuum the rug?"

Patrick smiled. "I just might," he said. "It could use it. And speaking of cleaning up, you could use a shave."

Pres ran his hand over his chin and shrugged.

"I'm serious," Patrick told him. "I thought I was doing this just to keep busy," he said, pointing to a trash bag. "But then I realized you wouldn't want Mary Ellen to come home to a disaster area, not after what she's been through. And she and Tara are going to come home, don't think they're not. It can't last much longer, Pres, it just can't. So you'd better do something about your chin, and fast, before you have a bird's nest growing there."

But Friday morning came, and as the cheerleaders gathered in the gym for their extra practice, nothing had changed.

CHAPTER

 13

"If you think we're down,
    Better think again!
    We're coming back
    And we're gonna win!"

Since the Wolves had won their last five games, the squad hadn't done this particular come-from-behind cheer in quite a while. That Friday morning, though, as they started to practice, the cheer fit their mood perfectly. Like they always did at a game when the Wolves were down, they were trying to convince themselves and everyone else that things would turn out fine.

"You see that score?
    Don't turn your back,
    'cause right behind you
    Is the big Wolf Pack!"

"What do you think?" Olivia asked, as Sean lifted her into the air.

"Haven't fallen on our faces yet," Sean said, setting her down and then springing into a back-flip.

"How do we look?" Peter asked Jessica as they stood together, stamping their feet and clapping their hands.

"Can't tell," Jessica answered. "It feels better, though."

Before the last verse, Olivia stepped out of line to take a look, since there was no one else around. Of all of them, Melissa had been the worst since they'd heard about Tara and Mary Ellen, and she was glad to see the alternate back in stride, as graceful as ever. Everyone was in step and on cue, she couldn't complain about that. Something was missing, but at the moment, she couldn't put her finger on what it was. Right now it was enough that they were working together again.

"Looking good!" she called out, and then ran back to join them for the end.

"When the game is done
And the ref yells stop!
The Tarenton Wolves
Will be the ones on top!"

"Good, but not perfect," Olivia commented when they finished. "We're not there yet. Let's try it again."

Without any hesitation, even from Sean, who usually protested at least once, the cheerleaders rearranged themselves and got ready to start the cheer all over.

"Hold it!" Everyone looked to see Ardith Engborg standing just inside the gym doors, a cup of coffee in one hand and her carryall bag in the other. She walked to the stands, set down her coffee and her bag, shrugged off her coat, and turned back to the squad. "I didn't want to miss it," she explained. "Now you can try again."

With the coach watching, the cheerleaders put even more effort into it, and when they finished, Coach Engborg looked almost satisfied.

"Some of you forgot to smile," she commented. "But technically, it was excellent. I know what all of you have been going through," she went on, "how worried you've been. I realize that's been the problem with your last few performances, and I certainly can't blame you. But I was afraid I was going to have to step in and do something — I didn't know what — to get you motivated again." She picked up her coat, bag, and coffee and smiled at them. "Now I can see you've managed to do that for yourselves. And I'm proud of you." Lowering her voice, she said softly, "Tara and Mary Ellen would be, too."

Then the coach's usual briskness returned, and as she strode towards the doors, she called back, "I expect you all here forty-five minutes before game time tonight. You can still use a good warm-up session!"

For Pres and Patrick, the day dragged on so slowly it seemed as if the earth were being rotated by hand. Patrick had picked up the plates and

138

cups and even gone so far as to dust the furniture so that the living room looked presentable again. Pres had shaved, showered, and put on a red, unwrinkled sweater, so he looked presentable, too. The cleanup had taken all of an hour, and when they were finished, there seemed nothing more to do but sit and wait and watch the clouds roll in.

"Looks like we're in for a storm," Sergeant Wells commented, eyeing the darkening sky. "I hope it's just rain, not snow. You never can tell this time of year."

"Rain," Patrick said. "According to this morning's paper, we're going to get rain, lightning, thunder, the works. It's five now; the storm's supposed to hit in about an hour."

Pres stood up and started for the kitchen, not interested in a discussion of the weather. As he passed Inspector Albright, she slammed down her phone and jumped out of her chair, her eyes bright with excitement.

"The van?" Pres asked quickly.

"The van," she said. "We think we've found it."

Patrick and the sergeant were on their feet, too, now, waiting for the details.

"It's parked in an alley between Cadman and Cooper Streets," the inspector said. "It's not a bad area of town, just a little run-down. But it's being slowly built back up, and that means lots of movement — some people leaving and others coming in."

"So nobody would be suspicious of some newcomers," Pres said.

The inspector nodded. "And these aren't

houses with big yards or anything. They're more like townhouses you find in a city, and most of them have been divided up into two or three apartments. That would make it easier on the kidnappers, too."

"What about the van?" Patrick asked. "What happens now?"

"Now is when we have to be the most careful," Inspector Albright told him. "Cadman and Cooper have plenty of houses on them. We have to find out which one the van goes with, and we have to do it without making anybody nervous."

"Is it the only car in the alley?" the sergeant asked.

"No, there are a lot of others. The houses don't have garages and the people use the street or the alleys."

"Accident?" the sergeant suggested.

"I thought of that," the inspector agreed.

"What are you talking about?" Pres asked.

"We get one of our people to drive down the alley and put a dent in the van," Sergeant Wells said. "The timing would be right because it'll be dark soon and the alley probably isn't well lighted. Then, naturally, our man's got to find out who the van belongs to because he's got to call his insurance company and — "

The sergeant's explanation was cut short by the ringing of the telephone, and as Pres hurried to answer he found himself hoping it was a wrong number. He wanted to hear more about the van. He wanted to know exactly how they planned to find the owner without putting Mary Ellen and Tara in more danger. He still didn't completely

trust the police and he had to make sure they were
were going to be super-careful.

But it wasn't a wrong number. As he heard the
familiar voice, Pres couldn't help wondering if
the man had a sixth sense.

"Are you listening, Mr. Tilford?"

"Yes."

"You have the money?"

"That's what I told you the last time you
called," Pres said.

"Then here are the rules of the game. We want
you to — "

"Not until I talk to Mary Ellen and Tara,"
Pres interrupted. "Those are my rules."

"Don't get smart, Mr. Tilford."

"Don't get stupid," Pres shot back. "Just get
Mary Ellen and Tara."

The line went dead.

Pres hung up the phone but kept a tight grip on
the receiver. He looked like he was thinking about
ripping the phone from the wall, but before anyone had a chance to move or speak, the phone
rang again, and Pres had the receiver to his ear
before the sound stopped.

"Pres, it's me," Mary Ellen said. "I'm okay.
I'm still okay."

Pres waited.

"I'm all right, too," Tara said, and Patrick felt
his heartbeat triple in speed as he heard her voice
over the speaker. She sounded tired, he thought,
and drowsy, the same way she'd sounded when
she fell asleep that night on the phone.

By this time, the kidnapper was back on the
line. "You satisfied, Mr. Tilford?"

"Yes."

"Good. Then listen. I'll tell you this once, so get it right. You put the money in a canvas bag, and in half an hour you get in your car and drive to the library. You park there, take the bag, and walk to the phone booth at the end of the parking lot. You'll get a call at 6:35. Be there."

Once more, the line went dead. Pres hung up and looked at the inspector. "What now?" he asked, his voice low and tense.

"Now you do as he said," she told him. "Thirty minutes isn't enough time for us to stage anything with the van. We have people watching it, of course, and they'll stay there. But this isn't a time for us to do anything but watch. You heard him — he sounded wound up as tight as a spring. He's scared. If we started asking questions about the van now, it would be too dangerous."

Pres nodded. Not only did it make sense, but it was what he'd wanted to do from the beginning. Now that the time had come, though, he was terrified.

"I know you're frightened, but you can do it," Inspector Albright said, as if she'd read his thoughts. Except for the first time they'd met, when she'd shaken his hand, she hadn't touched him. She'd been polite, friendly, and businesslike. Efficient, that's how Pres thought of her. But now, as she reached out and put a hand on his shoulder, he realized that Inspector Albright was truly on his side in this.

"Sure I can do it," he said. "Come on, let's find a canvas bag, so I can be ready. Let's get Mary Ellen and Tara back." He managed a smile for the inspector. "If we're lucky, maybe we'll even get the bad guys, too."

In spite of the brave words, Pres was still terrified when he left the house and drove toward the library. He felt completely alone, and after finally discovering he was glad to have the police on his side, he wanted them there now, too.

By the time he reached the library parking lot, the rain had started. He still had ten minutes before the call was supposed to come but rather than wait in the car and take a chance on missing it, he walked to the phone booth and squeezed himself inside. The bag of money was on the floor between his feet, and as he looked down at it, he hoped nobody decided to rob him tonight.

It was almost closing time; people were coming out of the library and heading for their cars or the bus stop. Most of them hadn't been prepared for the rain, in spite of the forecast, and as Pres looked nervously up and down the street, he saw an elderly woman holding a newspaper over her head and hurrying toward the phone booth.

Pres had been brought up to be polite and thoughtful, especially to elderly people who were getting drenched. But this time, he didn't have to think twice. He squeezed himself as far into the phone booth as possible, slid the door almost shut, grabbed the receiver, and started an enthusiastic conversation with an imaginary person, keeping one finger on the hook and hoping the woman wouldn't notice.

After standing and staring pointedly at him for five long minutes, the woman finally heaved a big sigh and stalked off, shaking her head at his rudeness. Pres checked his watch. Five more minutes.

When the phone rang, it rang exactly on time. Pres heaved his own sigh — at least they hadn't kept him waiting.

"Good, Mr. Tilford. Are you ready for the next step?"

"Yes."

"You'll walk twenty blocks east until you come to an all-night diner. The phone booth's right inside the door. Be ready to answer it at 7:45."

"That's almost an hour," Pres protested. "I can be there in fifteen minutes. What am I supposed to do while I wait?"

"Have some coffee in the diner," the kidnapper suggested.

"Can't you call sooner?"

"Just do as we say, Mr. Tilford. And don't forget you're not alone. Somebody's watching you every minute. So don't do anything stupid."

Zipping up his jacket, Pres took a tight hold of the bag's handles and then stepped out into the rain.

Just about the time that Pres was ordering a cup of hot coffee in the all-night diner, the cheerleaders and the pompon squad were moving onto the floor to do the routine they'd bungled so badly at the girls' basketball game. Even though she knew they were back on track, Olivia found herself crossing her fingers that they wouldn't blow it this time, too.

She didn't have to worry. Moving with precision, the cheerleaders led the pompon squad through the intricate routine as if it were the simplest thing they'd ever done. Nobody turned the wrong way, nobody missed a step, their movements were crisp and strong. And when they were finished, and the teams took the floor, the fans greeted them with a cheer that almost covered the noise of the thunder outside.

Something was still missing, Olivia knew that. They'd been fine technically, but she knew the heart was gone, and probably wouldn't be back until Tara and Mary Ellen were safe. But Coach Engborg looked pleased, and even Diana couldn't find anything to complain about. "I see you've been practicing," she commented to Olivia and Jessica as they filed off the floor.

Olivia ignored her, but Jessica laughed. "You mean you're admitting we were good?" she asked Diana.

"Well, I don't mind admitting that," Diana said. "Why should I? After all, when you look good, I look good."

Jessica laughed, and when Olivia asked her what was so funny, she said, "We performed like robots. Our hearts still aren't in it, didn't you notice?"

Olivia nodded. "But I still don't get the joke."

"The joke," Jessica explained, "is that Diana couldn't tell the difference."

CHAPTER

The second set of instructions Pres received turned out to be the last. From the diner, he was to take another walk, this time to a movie theatre a few blocks away. Once there, he was to buy a ticket and find a seat in the third row from the back. After exactly fifteen minutes, he was to get up and go, leaving the canvas bag underneath the seat.

Pres had barely tasted the three cups of coffee he'd had at the diner, but now, as he walked to the theatre, he was glad for their warmth. The wind had picked up, whipping his hair and jacket and driving the rain against his face so hard it felt like hail. Bolts of lightning and cracks of thunder were so bright and loud it seemed like the Fourth of July.

By the time Pres reached the theatre, he was cold and soaked. With numb fingers he paid for a ticket, then stepped inside the deserted lobby.

"Remember, we're with you," the kidnapper had said, and Pres had an almost overwhelming urge to look back at the street to see if someone else had suddenly decided to go to a movie that was already half over.

Fighting down the urge, Pres hitched the bag of money up a little higher and walked into the darkened theatre. He waited a few seconds for his eyes to adjust, then walked down the sloping aisle to the third row from the back.

Except for a man sitting at the very end, toward the far wall, the row was empty. Is that him? Pres wondered. The man seemed completely engrossed in the movie, his hand dipping automatically in and out of a popcorn box. Pres stood there watching him so long that someone in the row behind whispered loudly for him to sit down. He sat in the aisle seat, leaving ten empty chairs between them. If that was the guy, Pres didn't want to make it easy for him.

Pres never noticed what the movie was. He heard the crowd laughing from time to time, but he never took his eyes off the glowing blue clock over the exit door. In exactly fifteen minutes, he stood up, wedged the bag under the seat, and walked back up the aisle.

"If you want to see your wife and her friend again," the kidnapper had said, "you'll walk straight outside and get far away from that theatre as fast as you can. Don't look back, Mr. Tilford."

Pres didn't hang around and he didn't look back. In just a few minutes he was blocks away from the movie theatre, far enough, he thought, to slow down and take a breather. He wasn't tired, but he was so keyed up he was almost gasping.

But it wasn't a good night for a stroll. The storm was really hitting its stride now, and Pres heard signs clanking and saw a few people rushing for shelter. His own shelter was miles away and his car wasn't much closer. Hunching his shoulders against the rain and wind, he picked up his pace again.

He'd gone one more block when a car pulled up to the curb, soaking his pants to the knees with a fine, muddy spray. Pres jumped back anyway, and just as he did, the car door flew open.

"Get in!" Inspector Albright shouted over a clap of thunder.

Pres didn't need to be told twice. Inside the car, he found Patrick in the backseat and Sergeant Wells at the wheel, and before he'd completely closed the door, the sergeant was pulling the car back onto the street.

"How did you find me?" Pres asked. "You couldn't have tapped every public phone in Tarenton."

The inspector glanced back at him in surprise. "You really didn't think we'd let you make that trip alone, did you?"

"You mean you were following me?"

"Well, not the sergeant and me," she said. "But others in the department were. Undercover, of course," she added, before he had a chance to ask.

"I should have known," Pres said. Then he started to tell them about his ransom journey, but stopped before he'd finished the first sentence. "Wait a minute, if somebody was following me, maybe they saw the kidnapper come out of the theatre."

"They did," Inspector Albright told him. "We got the call about five minutes ago. He's on his way to the Cadman Street area now, and our people are already in place, waiting for him."

"What about us?" Pres asked, his heart pounding in his ears. "Where are we going?"

The inspector glanced at him again, smiling this time. "The same place. We're almost at the end of this, and I'm not going to miss it."

Pres looked at Patrick and saw that he was as scared and hopeful as he was. Was it really almost over?

Tara woke up with a start. "What's happening?" she asked. "I heard something loud."

"It's a storm," Mary Ellen said, turning from the window. "That was thunder you heard. It sounds really bad. There's lots of lightning and it's pouring out there." She pulled on her jacket. "It makes me cold just to hear it."

"Me, too," Tara said, sitting up and swinging her legs over the side of the bed. "Maybe our 'waiter' will bring us tea this time. Tea would taste good."

"It sure would," Mary Ellen agreed ruefully. "But I don't think we're going to get any dinner tonight."

"Why not? Not that I could eat it," Tara said, "but why wouldn't he bring dinner? He hasn't missed a meal yet."

"I don't know, but it's eight-thirty and he still hasn't come." Another roar of thunder made

Mary Ellen jump and move closer to the bed. "I wish that would stop," she said. "My nerves are in bad enough shape already."

Tara's head ached and she pressed her hands against it, hoping that would help. It didn't. Maybe if she splashed her face with cold water, she thought. She stood up to walk into the bathroom, and just as she stepped in front of Mary Ellen, they both heard the key in the door.

The door swung open, the man walked in, sidestepped the two girls, and headed for the low table where he always put their food. He'd just bent down when there was a loud crack, as if something huge and wooden had been split in two, and then the lights went out. For a few seconds, before the next flash of lightning, the room was in total darkness.

It was as if the two girls had planned it. They reached out at the same time, grabbed hands, and sped out the door. A left turn would have taken them to the room where they'd made the phone calls, so they turned right, running quickly down a hallway that ended in a door.

Mary Ellen fumbled for the knob, wanting to scream, knowing it would be locked. But it wasn't, and by the time they heard the man's footsteps behind them, they were out the door and halfway down a staircase, leaning on the bannister to keep from falling.

When they reached the bottom of the stairs, another lightning bolt brightened the sky, sending enough light into the building for Tara and Mary Ellen to see another door. And this one had a glass panel in it. This door led outside.

The man was on the stairs now, they could hear his footsteps clattering down. Both girls reached for the door, wrenched it open, and burst outside, still clasping each other's hands.

Then other hands were reaching for them, pushing them to the side, shoving them down to the wet pavement. But before they could scream, they heard someone say, "Police. Just stay down. You'll be all right."

Half an hour later, when Inspector Albright said they could go, Pres found it hard to let Mary Ellen out of his arms even for the time it would take to get in the car.

"There'll be a lot more questions, of course, and we'll want a statement from you," the inspector said, "but for now, I think you should go home and try to relax."

"That won't be easy," Mary Ellen said. "I'm still shaking and it's not from the cold."

"I know." The inspector looked sympathetic. "But you don't have to worry about those two again. We got one of them chasing you down the stairs and the other one putting your husband's bag of money in the van. I'd say the evidence is pretty well stacked against them."

Mary Ellen looked up at the house where she'd spent so many long hours. The storm had worn itself out, the electricity was back on, and in the glow of the streetlights, she could see that it was just an ordinary-looking house. "I still can't believe we were right here in Tarenton." She shivered again and looked at Pres. "I still can't believe it's over."

"It is," Pres assured her. "Take my word for it. Better yet, take Inspector Albright's word for it. She knows this business a lot better than I do."

It was a compliment, and the inspector smiled and shook his hand before walking back to her own car.

"She was great," Pres said. "I fought her tooth and nail at the beginning. I even fought Patrick because I was so scared to let the police in on it. Now I'm glad I did."

Mary Ellen leaned against him. "Tara and I fought, too," she told him. "She wanted to try to escape and I told her she was crazy. But when the lights went out, I didn't even have to think. I just grabbed her hand and ran."

"The arguing doesn't matter anymore," Pres said, holding her tight. "You two are safe, that's what matters. I guess even people who are close don't always see eye to eye."

He pulled her close again, never wanting to let her go, feeling his throat close up with emotion. For the first time since the whole horrible ordeal had started, Mary Ellen stopped being strong, just for a minute. Her eyes filled with tears.

Then she laughed, shakily, suddenly remembering. "See this?" she said, pointing to the orange button on her jacket.

" 'Love Beats All,' " Pres read aloud.

"I bought it Saturday, right before . . . before it happened," she said. "We argued about the party, remember? I was going to wear it to let you know we could argue as much as we want, but we'd both win, because we love each other."

Pres kissed her. He had no argument with that at all.

"Are you sure you don't need to go to the hospital?" Patrick asked again, as the police car drove them toward Tara's house. He was holding both of Tara's hands in his, and he couldn't take his eyes off her.

"I'm sure," Tara said. "I'm feeling a little better, especially now that we're out of that horrible place. Anyway, I can always see my doctor if I need to. But I'm sure I won't. It's just the flu, that's all."

"It's the what?"

"The flu," Tara said. "What are you laughing at? Believe me, there's nothing funny about the flu. And I look horrible!"

Patrick laughed again, pulling her close to him. "You've never looked so good to me," he said. "And I'm not laughing at that. It's just that when we found out what had happened to you, your parents wanted to know what to tell people, since it had to be kept secret. So Inspector Albright suggested the flu."

Tara laughed, too, her headache forgotten for a moment. "Well, I know Melissa did a great job filling in for me, so I won't worry about that," she said. "But Coach Engborg gets impatient when one of us just has the sniffles. And I've been out seven days with the flu? She must be furious!"

"No, she knows what really happened," Patrick said. "The whole squad does. Pres and I wanted them to know, because they care about you and Mary Ellen so much."

Tara leaned against him. "They must have been miserable," she said. "I would have been."

"We all were," Patrick told her. "But you know the squad — they've been cheering for you all the way." And he pulled her closer, if that was possible — safe next to his heart.

There were twenty minutes left on the clock. The Tarenton Wolves were ahead by twelve points, and from the looks of the Garrison team, the Wolves could have sat out the rest of the game and still won.

"I wouldn't mind if somebody just moved the clock ahead." Sean said, as the cheerleaders gathered for a quick break. "For once, I'd like to get out of here."

"Just a few more minutes," Olivia said. "I know how you feel, but hang in there."

Everyone understood how Sean felt, because they all felt the same way. Even though they'd been good tonight, even though the routines had been almost flawless, nobody really felt like cheering. They were going through the motions, and thanks to their meeting the day before, they were good enough to fool almost everyone. But they couldn't fool themselves, and performing like automatons brought them no joy at all.

"What shall we do next?" Hope asked unenthusiastically.

"It doesn't matter," Peter said. "Let's just make it short. I'm tired of smiling."

Melissa started to suggest a cheer, then stopped as she saw Coach Engborg in the doorway. "Look!" she said, pointing. "Something's happened! Look at her face!"

The crowd had started its own cheer, but the squad paid no attention. Ardith Engborg rarely even grinned, but now, as she hurried along the sidelines to the cheerleaders, she was positively beaming.

"It's over!" she called out while she was still a few feet away. "They're safe, both of them."

The cheerleaders, oblivious to the game and the crowd, threw their arms up in triumph and then started hugging everyone in sight, including the coach.

"Who did it?" Sean asked.

"I don't have many details," Coach Engborg said, her cheeks pink with excitement. "Just two men who wanted a lot of money. And the van you saw was the one," she told him. "Inspector Albright said to thank you again."

"Great!" Sean picked up Jessica and twirled her around. "They're back, isn't that great?"

"Hey, you guys!" someone in the crowd shouted. "We might be ahead but the game's not over yet. How about a cheer?"

"Good idea," the coach said, regaining some of her composure. "I know you're excited, but we do have a game to finish."

Still laughing, the cheerleaders dashed onto the floor, and none of them were surprised when Olivia started the come-from-behind cheer.

* * *

"If you think we're down,
    Better think again!
    We're coming back
    And we're gonna win!"

The crowd was slightly mystified at first, since the Wolves were so far ahead, but it wasn't long before they joined in at the top of their lungs. With Tara and Mary Ellen back, the cheerleaders were back, too, and this time, they were cheering their hearts out.

Tara finds out it isn't the truth that hurts . . . it's the lies! Read Cheerleaders #43, TELLING LIES.